Slowly and silently Philby rose to his feet. Longarm could make out his companion's form a bit more clearly now, and there was no mistaking the movement of Philby's arm as he drew his revolver from its hip holster. He began a careful advance toward the bedroll where Longarm lay watching.

Philby reached a point directly opposite Longarm. Only the small irregular circle of coals left by the dead camp fire separated them. Without taking his eyes off Longarm, Philby brought up his weapon slowly, his head canted to one side as he bent forward to get his eyes level with the revolver's sights.

Longarm did not have the amount of time Philby spent in taking careful aim, nor did he need it at such close range. He tilted his Colt's muzzle and at the same time swiveled the barrel. His shot broke the night's silence only a fraction of a second before Philby closed his finger on the trigger of his own weapon, but that was time enough.

TABOR EVANS

LONGARM

AND THE LONGLEY LEGEND

JOVE BOOKS, NEW YORK

LONGARM AND THE LONGLEY LEGEND

A Jove Book/published by arrangement with
the author

PRINTING HISTORY
Jove edition / November 1990

ISBN: 0-515-10445-0

Jove Books are published by The Berkley Publishing Group,
200 Madison Avenue, New York, New York 10016.
The name "Jove" and the "J" logo
are trademarks belonging to Jove Publications, Inc.

PRINTED IN THE UNITED STATES OF AMERICA

10 9 8 7 6 5 4 3 2 1

Chapter 1

Longarm strained his eyes and drew his brows together as he tried to look beyond the wide bend in the trail ahead. During his long service as a lawman he'd learned that the lawless who preyed on passing travelers favored such curved spots for ambushing the unwary. His horse had already started swerving onto the beginning of a long sweeping curve that obscured the pathway ahead, and Longarm persisted in his effort to look along the rutted and hoof-dented strip of beaten earth, but he could find no gaps in the high growth of scrub mesquite and spindling, thinly leafed huisache trees that grew thickly along the edges of the narrow trail and formed an almost impenetrable screen.

Even the advantage of height given him by being in the saddle instead of on foot was not enough to allow Longarm's eyes to pierce the shield of barely moving leaves and branches. Putting a small amount of pressure on the reins with his left hand, Longarm dropped his right hand to the butt of his holstered Colt. Responding to the tightening of its reins, the big bay livery horse was already beginning to slow its pace. It slowed even more as it reached the furrowed ground of the curve, and the ruts in the path caused an occasional small misstep.

"Them damn bushes hides things better'n any old maid's window shade," Longarm muttered in a half whisper into the silent air as he kept trying again to peer ahead.

For a moment this effort to look more than a dozen or so yards in front of him was as useless as his earlier one had been. He was about to return his attention to the ground when he saw two or three of the spindly-topped saplings beyond the bend quivering while those around them remained motionless.

"Old son, that wasn't no wind making them trees move," he told himself. "A wind would've put all of 'em to shaking. Sure as God made little green apples, there's somebody up ahead there."

Despite his deduction, Longarm did not tighten the reins to slow his horse. He let the bay keep up the pace it had been maintaining during the two or three hours since its last rest stop, but now Longarm paid more attention to the treetops than he did to the treacherous rutted ground. He saw the treetops quiver once more, then settle down. By this time he could see that he was close to the end of the sweeping bend, for on his right side he could see twenty or thirty yards of the bordering vegetation and a long, narrow triangular section of the trail itself.

Then Longarm's keen eyes triggered his equally keen reflexes as he saw an arm and shoulder of someone standing in the center of the rutted pathway. His response was

2

automatic. Only a few seconds after he'd seen the arm and shoulder, Longarm's Colt was drawn and ready.

"Oh, no! Don't shoot!" a woman's voice called. "Please! Please stop! I need a little bit of help!"

By the time the woman's voice had died away, Longarm's horse had covered the last bit of the curved stretch, and now Longarm could see her clearly. She was standing beside the road, a dozen or so yards ahead. Her arm was still raised to wave, but she let it drop when Longarm somewhat sheepishly holstered his Colt while he was covering the last few yards that separated them.

"I'm right sorry if I spooked you a mite, ma'am," he said as he doffed his flat-crowned Stetson. "But all I could see of you at first was your shoulder and arm."

"Well, that makes me feel better," she said. "When I saw your gun, I was a little bit—"

"Spooked, like I said," Longarm broke in. "Well, you don't need to worry none, ma'am. I'm a deputy United States marshal. My name's Long, Custis Long. Thing is, on a crooked trail like this one, it ain't always safe for a man in a job like mine to go around a blind corner where he's just seen signs somebody's waiting. The way this trail winds, I couldn't tell whether you was a man or a woman, and in most places in the backwoods like this there's likely to be a few men that don't take real friendly to a lawman."

"Yes, I know." She nodded. "I'm Lisa Ross. My wagon's broken down and I've been waiting here for— well, I'm sure it just seems longer than it's really been. But nobody's passed by, and I was beginning to think about unhitching my wagon mule and riding it to the nearest town when I heard you coming."

As they talked, Longarm and the young woman had

3

been examining one another. Longarm placed her as being in her middle or late twenties. She had on a bar-checked black and red calico blouse and a blue poplin skirt. Both were faded and bore signs of having been much worn. Her shoes were over-the-ankle button-ups, their black leather surfaces scraped and battered. Her hat was a narrow-brimmed woven straw which shaded her face without concealing it.

There was nothing especially notable about her face; it was lightly tanned and her features were regular. Her eyes were dark brown, and the few strings of hair that looped down below the brim of her hat were somewhere in the range between dark brown and black. She was neither ugly nor beautiful, but in the broad range of looks called attractive.

"I got to give you credit for spunk," Longarm told her. "Hitting out by yourself on a back road like this one. I reckon that's right about me guessing there's nobody with you?"

"Yes, of course that's right. If I'd had anybody to help me fix my wagon, I'd be on my way to town right now."

"Which town might it be you're heading for?"

"Circleville," she replied. "But I don't suppose you've ever heard of it."

"You sure suppose right. Just guessing, I'd say it's between here and Austin?"

"Yes." Lisa nodded. "It's not on the main road, though. It's off the road along a sort of trace that cuts off just past Walburg. I've got some relatives in Circleville that I'm going to live with until I can decide what to do."

Longarm could gather from the manner of her reply

that the trip she was making marked the termination of a marriage that had ended with either the desertion or death of her husband. He asked no questions, but nodded before going on. "I reckon you're sorta anxious to get moving again."

"Of course I am! I'd like to get to Circleville before it gets dark."

"It looks like what I better do is see about fixing up your wagon so's you can be on your way."

"You'd be doing me a real big favor, Marshal Long."

While Lisa spoke, Longarm had been swinging out of his saddle. He went on. "Now, you just show me where that wagon is. After I've had a look at it, I'll know in a jiffy whether or not I can fix it."

"It's just a little ways back along that trace," she said. "But I'm not sure what's wrong with it is fixable. I'm afraid the back axletree's broken."

"Don't give up till I've had a chance to find out for sure," Longarm advised. "I've found out that things has got a way of looking worse'n they are, first time you see 'em. If bad comes to worse, I can give you a lift to the next town, where there'd likely be a blacksmith shop."

A few more paces brought them in sight of the broken wagon. It was heavily loaded, sagging on one side, the horse still in the shafts. Longarm saw at a glance that the arched rear axle frame was indeed broken; a long jagged crack ran from one side of its center arch to the wheel socket. A loop of rope hung from the wagon's whip socket. Longarm indicated it with a gesture.

"That's all we'll need to fix the axle," he said. "But I'll need a lever to lift the wagon with, and there's plenty of little trees alongside the road here, but I don't carry an ax with me."

5

"There's a hatchet under the seat," Lisa told him. "Will that do?"

"Sure. I don't need such a much of a tree, just one that's stout enough to use for a lever. We can pile up some rocks in back of the wagon that'll make a sorta pivot for it."

"Shouldn't we unload the wagon first?"

While they talked, Longarm had been studying the wagon and its contents. Now he shook his head as he replied. "We might have to do that if push comes to shove, but let's try first and see if we can't get by without going to all that trouble. Now, if you'll just hand me your hatchet, I'll chop down one of them little saplings over yonder and we'll get started."

"Surely there's something I can do to help you," Lisa said.

"Oh, sure. Soon as I take down that little tree over yonder, you can trim the branches off of it while I'm piling up some of them flat rocks in back of the wagon."

For the next few minutes both Longarm and Lisa worked diligently. By the time Lisa had trimmed the limbs off the sapling Longarm chopped down, he'd piled a dozen or more of the large flat stones that littered the roadside into a pyramid a pace or two behind the damaged wagon's tailgate.

"There!" Lisa said. She laid the hatchet aside and lifted the sapling's trimmed trunk to stand it erect. "That's the last limb. If you're ready for the pole, it's ready for you."

Longarm looked up from testing the rock pyramid he'd been busy building. He gave the center of the piled stones an experimental kick, and nodded his satisfaction as he said, "This oughta hold long enough to do the job.

6

Now, if you'll hand me that hank of rope yonder, we'll see if this job's going to work the way I figure it will. By rights, we oughta unload the wagon, but maybe we can get it off the ground. All we need to do is raise it an inch or two."

While he spoke, Longarm was unbuckling his gunbelt. He put it carefully on the wagon seat and covered it with his hat, then turned to Lisa. "I guess you've done figured out what I got in mind?"

"I think so. You're going to lever up the back end of the wagon and use some of my rope to wrap up the axle socket so that crack won't splinter out and break a wheel off."

"You hit square in the bull's-eye, ma'am. I figure if that split's fixed you'll be able to make it into Walburg without no more trouble, and there's likely a blacksmith shop there where they can do a proper job that'll last you."

"I believe you're right, Marshal Long," she agreed. "But don't you think we've gotten well enough acquainted by now to stop being so formal? I'm used to my friends calling me Lisa instead of just ma'am, and I'm sure yours call you—Custis, didn't you say?"

"Well, now," Longarm answered, "I ain't one to go by a lot of citified flimflam. Except there's one thing."

"And what is that?"

"Oh, I got a sorta nickname, and I answer to it a sight better'n I do to my real name."

"What is your nickname?"

"It's Longarm."

"Of course! The long arm of the law!" Lisa exclaimed. "We agree on the names then?"

"Why, sure." He smiled. "But instead of palavering, we oughta be getting your wagon fixed. If we don't work pretty fast and get that mend finished, it'll be plumb dark before you get to where you're going."

Stepping to the rear of the wagon, Longarm put the trimmed sapling in place, its butt below the long split in the axle, its center balanced on the heap of flat stones. He bent over the improvised lever and pushed down. It required all the effort Longarm could muster, but with an assortment of creaks and squeaks the wagon rose slowly, a fraction of an inch at a time, until both its rear wheels cleared the ground. The clearance was less than the span of a man's hand, but it was enough.

Turning his head toward Lisa, Longarm said, "You think you can sit on this pole and keep the wagon wheels from dropping back on the road while I fix up that axle?"

"I'm certainly willing to try," she said. "How long will it take you to do whatever it is you need to?"

"Not more'n a few minutes. All I aim to do is put some turns of rope around that split place in the axle frame. Then I'll pull it tight and lash it so it won't bust wide open."

"It seems to me that you've got it all figured out," Lisa told him. "If you're ready to start your repair job, just tell me what you want me to do besides sitting on the pole."

"That's the long and short of it," Longarm assured her.

Lisa stepped up to him and lowered herself to the improvised lever. Slowly and carefully, Longarm stood up and looked at the sapling. Even when it was arched into a curve it seemed solidly in place.

Taking the end of the rope, he crawled under the wagon bed. At close range, the damaged axle frame looked worse than he'd anticipated. Longarm began his wrapping several inches from one end of the split, and carried it in carefully even spirals past the opposite end of the break. Then he reversed his wrapping and tied off the rope. After he'd finished inspecting the mend he called to Lisa.

"Stand up real slow now. I'm going to stay here and see what happens to this axle frame when them back wheels takes on a full load."

Though the mended frame gave a creak or two as Lisa stood up and released the lever, it seemed solid enough when Longarm gave the winding rope a hard slap or two. Satisfied that he'd done the best job possible with the limited resources at hand, Longarm crawled back to the trail.

"I don't claim that'd stand up to a buckboard race," he told Lisa as he stood up. "But if we take it sorta slow and easy, it oughta last till the next town where there's a blacksmith shop."

"That'd be Walburg," she said. "And it's not very far. But from what you just said, I got the idea that you're going to ride with me, alongside the wagon."

"Well, now, you wouldn't expect me just to ride away from a lady that's in trouble. Besides, I got to go that way myself. But I been forking this nag for a long stretch. I don't reckon you'd mind if I was to hitch it to the tailgate and ride on into Walburg setting on the seat with you?"

"I not only wouldn't mind, Longarm, I'd be happy as a jaybird to have some company. This road's been so deserted all the way that I sometimes get the idea I'm the only one traveling on it."

"I'll just do that, then," Longarm said. "But it ain't only to be better company. If I'm setting in the wagon, I can feel it if that patching-up job starts getting unraveled.

If it does, the quicker I can get at fixing it again, the easier it'll be."

"I hadn't thought of that," she said. "But I can see your idea makes good sense. Swing up then, and we'll be on our way."

Longarm needed only a few moments to hitch his livery horse to the wagon's tailgate and settle down on the wagon seat beside Lisa. He lit one of his long slim cheroots and said, "If you want me to spell you at the reins . . ."

Lisa shook her head. "No, you've just done a very hard bit of work, and I'd better get used to the way this wagon feels with that mended axle."

"Then let's get on our way," Longarm said. "We won't be moving very fast, so I figure we'll hit that little town we're heading for just a smidgen after dark."

Darkness settled slowly on the humpy stretch of sparsely wooded prairie. There was still a tinge of sun glow in the west when they topped a long gentle upward slope and less than a half-mile ahead saw the yellowish twinkle of a town's lights glistening through the gathering gloom.

"That's Walburg!" Lisa exclaimed. "And with any luck we'll be there before the blacksmith shop closes up."

"One thing sure," Longarm observed. "We don't have to worry no longer about that axle giving way."

"I'm glad it's held up until we got here, but it certainly spoiled my plan to get all the way to Circleville today."

"Well, it ain't the end of the world," Longarm pointed out. He went on. "Now, we're just about in town, so we might as well just go on to the hotel. While you're getting settled in, I'll bring the wagon back to the blacksmith shop. You just leave it to me to get him started fixing up your wagon. After you've had a good night's rest you'll feel better finishing your trip tomorrow."

"You don't have to take all that trouble." Lisa frowned. "I'm used to doing little chores like that myself."

"And I'm used to helping folks that's having trouble." He smiled. "So we'll just say it's settled."

By this time the wagon had almost reached the blacksmith shop. Lisa turned to Longarm and said firmly, "Longarm, I'm going to stop at that blacksmith shop, so please don't try to stop me."

Before Longarm could protest Lisa was reining off the road onto the wheel-rutted stretch of ground in front of the shop. Inside, the ringing of a hammer on an anvil and the dancing red glow of the forge told them that the smith was still at work. Lisa hauled the leathers back and turned to look at Longarm.

"Now," she went on, "let's find out how long it's going to take for them to fix the axle, and how much it'll cost."

"If that's what you want to do," he agreed.

When they walked into the shop the blacksmith was still at his anvil, busy hammering. He nodded, pounded the cooling metal with a few more well-placed swings, then turned to them and said, "Evening, folks. You got something you need help with?"

Before Longarm could reply, Lisa said, "The back axle on my wagon out there's cracked. I wonder if you can fix it."

"Well, now, lady, I can tell you more about it after I look at it. Jist pull it up to the door, where I can see good, and I'll know in about two minutes."

"I'll move the wagon," Longarm volunteered quickly.

He stepped outside and led the wagon horse in a semicircle to bring the wagon to a halt in front of the smithy's door, where Lisa and the smith stood waiting. The blacksmith peered at the cracked wood of the axle frame for a moment, then straightened up.

"Why, that won't be such a much of a job," he said. "All that axle frame needs is a couple of bolts through that split place. Draw them bolts tight, it's good as new, last you another twenty years. Trouble is, I can't get around to doing it till I finish the job I'm working on. I promised I'd have it done this evening."

"But you think you can have it ready early in the morning?" Lisa asked. Before the smith could reply she asked another question. "And how much will it cost?"

"Cost you half a dollar, ma'am. And you and your man can be on your way by sunup."

Before Lisa could reply, Longarm said, "You got a deal, friend. I guess all that truck on the wagon's going to be safe?"

"Safe as houses," the smith replied. "I'll pull the rig into the shop before I leave, and put your wagon horse and the one you're leading in my stable out back. Won't cost you nothing extra."

"From what you said, I take it there's a hotel in town here?" Longarm asked.

"Oh, sure. The Bowie House. Just go right on along the road, you can't miss it."

"Thanks," Longarm said. He turned to Lisa. "If you need anything off the wagon, I'll be glad to get it for you, Lisa. I've got to take my rifle and saddlebags with us."

Lisa shook her head and said, "Thank you, Longarm, but I'll get along just fine."

They walked in silence along the road toward town. Most of the buildings along its single street were dark, but a streak of light stretched across the street near the town's center. As they drew closer they could see that the lights came from two sources.

One was a weather-beaten single-story building that got its identity from the light streaming from the top and bottom of its swinging doors. The other, a two-story brick structure directly across the street, had wide glass-paned windows spanning a pair of wide glass windows that bore the words BOWIE HOUSE.

"Looks like that's the place the blacksmith told us about," Longarm said.

Lisa glanced at it and nodded, then turned to Longarm. "I guess you run into just about anything and everything in your line of work," she said.

"Pretty much. There ain't no two cases I've worked that's been just exactly alike."

"Then I don't suppose you'll be surprised by what I'm going to say," she went on.

"Seeing as I don't know what you got in mind, I can't see much of a way to answer that," he answered with a frown. "Maybe you better go on and say it."

Lisa hesitated for a moment, then said, "I just wanted you to know that when we get to the hotel we'll only need one room. You see, Longarm, I'm going to be sleeping with you in your bed tonight."

Chapter 2

For a moment Longarm was speechless. He could only stare openmouthed at Lisa. Her invitation—or announcement—was far from being the first of its kind he'd received, even though others had usually come from women with whom he'd been acquainted for more than a few hours.

"You didn't feel like you had to say that because you're short of money, did you?" he asked.

"Of course not. And it's not a thank-you either." A frown grew on Lisa's face. "Do I look like the kind of woman who'd sell herself for the price of a hotel room?"

"No, Lisa, I got to admit you don't. I reckon that's why you've sorta taken me by surprise."

"Of course, if you don't want to accept my invitation—"

"Now, I never said that, or even thought about saying

15

it," Longarm protested. "And I sure ain't going to try to get you to change your mind."

"Don't worry, I won't." She smiled. "I decided that I'd enjoy being in bed with you when we'd gotten halfway here from where I'd stopped back on the trail. Now that I've said it, I'm a little bit surprised at myself, because this is the first time I've ever given a man such a bold-faced invitation."

"I got to give you credit for not being somebody that beats around the bush," Longarm said. "So let's just go on in and I'll sign the register and we'll start getting acquainted better."

"There's just one thing I'm going to ask you, Longarm," Lisa said as he turned to her after locking the door of the room on the hotel's second floor. "Blow out that lamp the hotel clerk insisted on giving us, and don't light it again unless you need it to undress by."

"Being in the dark don't worry me a bit," Longarm assured her. He stepped to the bureau and blew out the lamp. Then he stood motionless while his eyes were adjusting to the room's darkness as he added, "In the kinda job I got, night's just about the same as daytime to me."

"Good," she said. "It's not that I'm embarrassed or anything like that, but—well, if you're the kind of man I've taken you for, you'll understand."

Night-light, the glow from the saloon across the street as well as the quarter-moon and stars, was now outlining the edges of the window shades, and Longarm could see Lisa silhouetted as a dim form standing between the bureau and the windows. She'd already taken off her shoes and was now fumbling at the neck of her

16

calf-length dress. As Longarm began unbuckling his belt he saw her shrug out of the dress and let it slide to the floor.

Longarm had been busy levering out of his boots; now he made quick work of unbuttoning his shirt and tossing it aside. He pushed down his jeans and stepped away from them before beginning to unbutton his longjohns. Before he'd had time to drop them, Lisa moved away from the window and came to stand in front of him.

In the room's gloom Longarm could see her only as a white form outlined against the slivers of dim light that spilled in around the edges of the window shades. Even the half darkness did not hide the bulges of her breasts and the outline of their rosettes, or the curve of her hips broken by the dark triangle below and between them.

"Let me," Lisa said, extending her arms and closing her hands over his as he began shrugging out of the longjohns.

Dropping his hands, Longarm stood motionless while Lisa pushed the clinging balbriggans over his shoulders and freed his arms from the sleeves. Longarm's hands sought her breasts. He began caressing them with his callused fingertips, and small shivers shook her now and again as she continued tugging at the balbriggans, working the garment down Longarm's chest to his waist and hips.

Lisa's hands brushing against him as she worked were having their effect on Longarm. As she tugged the under-suit below his hips to his thighs, her hands and arms brushed against his burgeoning erection and she abandoned the under-suit at once.

Longarm had not slackened his fingering caresses while Lisa was busy stripping him, and his impatience had been increasing as Lisa's soft hands and arms brushed against him more and more often. He took the initiative now. Stepping out of his longjohns, he wrapped his arms around her and pulled her to him. As their bodies pressed close, Lisa groped to find his fully swollen erection and cradled it for a moment.

"Oh, my!" she whispered as she guided him. "You're more man than I expected. Don't make me wait any longer!" Urgency creeping into her whisper, she went on. "Now, Longarm! Now!"

Longarm was more than ready to respond. He lifted Lisa and swiveled around to take the single short half step that was needed to reach the bed. He waited for a moment until Lisa placed him. Then he leaned forward, allowing her weight to pull them down. They fell on the bed, and as they landed he completed his penetration.

When Longarm plunged, Lisa cried out, a throaty explosion of delight. She rolled her hips and brought them up to meet his lunge, then locked her heels around his back. He started thrusting, driving slowly and deeply. As their bodies met with a muffled fleshy thwacking at the end of each plunge, small cries of delight bubbled from her lips.

Longarm maintained his short-spaced driving until Lisa no longer loosed her throaty wordless cries at the apex of his drives, but merged them into an almost unbroken stream. He stopped then for a few moments and sought her lips. When breathlessness forced him to break their tongue-entwining kiss, she lay almost quiescent for the first few moments under his gentler strokes.

Longarm's drives mounted in a continuing steadiness until Lisa began to twitch again. Buried fully within her gently quivering softness, Longarm stopped thrusting for a moment. He found her lips. She opened them to meet his questing tongue with hers and held their kiss until he began driving again.

Lisa's response was quicker now, and more fervent. She dug her heels into Longarm's back to lift herself in the tempo of his driving. When he began to speed his penetrations, small bubbles of sound started bursting from her lips. Longarm was driving hard now in response to his own body signals as well those he was sensing in Lisa's wilder thrashing.

When her soft cries grew sharper and broke the night's quiet more and more often, Longarm recognized the change and sped his lunges into a deep rhythmic driving. Lisa's cries were no longer intermittent; a single babble of incoherent sound streamed from her throat. Her body was tense and her thrashings wilder as Longarm drove to their final climax.

A sharp, high-pitched happy cry broke from Lisa's lips and Longarm silenced it with his own climactic thrust. He let her quivering form take his full weight to bury himself deeper, then lay motionless until the rippling tremors that were shaking both of them peaked and faded and they lay quietly, panting and spent.

For a long while neither Longarm nor Lisa moved. When she stirred gently and exhaled a long-trailing happy sigh, Longarm moved to lie beside her. A few more moments passed in silence before Lisa said, "I'm gladder than ever that I listened to my instinct instead of common sense, Longarm."

"I take that as a nice compliment, Lisa," he replied. "And I reckon I'm as glad as you are."

"From what you told me while we were on the way

19

here, you've gone quite a bit out of your way, helping me. I hope you won't get into trouble by spending so much time away from your job."

"That ain't nothing for neither one of us to worry about," Longarm assured her. "My chief up in Denver knows I like to wind up whatever case I'm on soon as I can, and I finished this one up a lot faster'n I figured. A day one way or the other won't make much—" He broke off as a raucous medley of shouts fractured the quiet night.

"It sounds like a fight down in the street," Lisa said.

"Likely it is. I guess you seen that saloon right across from the hotel."

"Yes. Probably some of the customers got into a drunken argument and decided the only way they could settle it was with their fists."

"I'll take a quick look from the window."

Longarm was getting out of bed as he spoke. He stepped to the window and pulled the shade away to peer outside. There were only four men on the street in front of the saloon, and his first glance was enough to see that two of them were holding the other two, obviously trying to keep them from turning their shouting match into a fistfight. While he was watching, several others pushed through the batwings and stood on the steps, waiting to see if the argument was going to end in a fight.

As close as he was now to the windowpane, Longarm could hear bits and snatches of the profanely shouted exchange between the two men who were being held apart. They were still struggling to get at one another, and he could see that unless one or both succeeded in breaking free, it was quite likely that the argument was going to continue for a while.

20

"Them old roosters down there ain't going to cool off for quite a spell," Longarm told Lisa as he turned away from the window. He was reaching for his trousers as he spoke. "And we sure don't want 'em raising cain for another hour or so. It'll only take a minute for me to settle their hash. All I got to do is go down and show my badge. It's the quickest way I can figure to stop their ruckus."

"I suppose you'd better do it then," she agreed. "It would be nice to have the rest of the night quiet, even if I don't think we'll be doing too much sleeping."

Longarm had already shrugged into his shirt and was stepping into his boots. He picked up his gunbelt and strapped it on as he started for the door. Over his shoulder, he said to Lisa, "This ain't going to keep me away but a minute."

Buttoning his shirt and trousers as he went down the stairs, Longarm buckled on his gunbelt and stepped out to the street. The argument in front of the saloon was still going on and showed no signs of subsiding. Two or three of the men who'd been trying to act as peacemakers were now joining in the argument between the pair they'd been restraining.

Longarm slid his wallet from his pocket and opened it as he crossed the street. When he reached the quarreling men he held the wallet up for them to see his badge. The first one in the small knot of onlookers who noticed it called out, "You damn fools, stop your yelling! You've brought out the law and we'll all be in trouble if you don't tame down!"

"Now, I don't aim to arrest nobody," Longarm said loudly. He waited until the small group had grown quiet and the pair who'd been arguing so loudly had calmed down. Then he went on. "There's folks in the hotel over yonder that's trying to sleep, and this ain't no time or place for you men to start a fracas."

One of the men who'd been holding back the arguing pair spoke up. "Maybe the lawman can settle this fuss, Tobe. He'd oughta know something about old Wild Bill Longley. Every man in this part of the country that ever wore a badge was after him at one time or another."

"How about it, Mister Lawman?" the man called Tobe asked. "Did you ever run across old Wild Bill?"

Longarm had recognized the Longley name. During his early days as a lawman he'd seen it on more wanted flyers than he could count. He shook his head as he replied, "I never met up with him. The only Wild Bill I ever met was Hickok, and that was after he started traveling with the circus. But I've heard about Wild Bill Longley, even if he was a mite before my time. He's the only one I ever heard of that walked away from his own hanging."

"That's right," one of the pair who'd been arguing so bitterly said quickly. "I was farming over by Giddings when they had that lynching bee and I seen him strung up with my own eyes. I didn't wait afterward to watch 'em cut him down, but everybody I talked to that was there swears he was dead when they cut him down that day."

"And that shows how damn much you know about it, Gabe!" his recent adversary snapped. "All you got to go by is what somebody told you who didn't know his tailbone from a hot rock! The hanging Wild Bill Longley walked away from was in Karnes County!"

"Maybe so, Ponch. But he was dead in Giddings, later on!" Gabe broke in. "And I know he was dead, damn it! I was there and you wasn't, so you—"

22

"You two! You, Ponch and Gabe!" a gruff voice broke in as the batwings swung open and light streamed out of the saloon to silhouette the aproned form of the barkeeper. "Before you get into a fracas that'll give my place a bad name, if all of you come inside to do your fussing and quit raising a ruckus out here on the street, your first drink'll be on the house!"

"Well, now!" Ponch observed. A grin was in his voice even though his face was still hidden by the night's shadow. "I don't guess any of you yahoos is about to say no to that. It ain't frequent when Old Fess pours a drink without he sees money first." Turning to Longarm, he said, "You better come along, friend. A free drink ain't nothing to sneeze at."

Longarm thought of Lisa, waiting in the hotel room. He decided almost instantly that the evening was still young and his parched throat deserved a few minutes of attention. He followed the men through the batwings and joined them at the bar.

When he saw them clearly for the first time, Longarm's first thought was that all of them were old enough to have been youths when Wild Bill Longley was at the peak of his lawless bloodletting career as a short-tempered trigger-happy killer. The two who'd been arguing, Ponch and Gabe, could have been twins. Both wore often-mended bib overalls, faded and streaked from being laundered in a tub of boiling water generously laced with homemade soft soap, and the faces of each of them were deeply tanned, dirt-streaked, and badly in need of a razor's attention. Gabe was a bit older than the others; his bristly growth of stubble was almost all white.

Lined up at the bar, the little group waited in silence while the barkeep set out shotglasses and filled them

from a bar bottle. When he reached Longarm, he squinted at him curiously for a moment before pouring; then as
he leaned across the scarred bar top to fill the shotglass
he said, "I ain't seen you around here before. Stranger
passing through, I reckon?"

"Just going outa my way a little bit to help a lady that
was having trouble with her wagon," Longarm replied.
He saw no need to reopen a discussion of his status as
a lawman. "Your friends started making a lot of noise
and keeping me awake, so I come across from the hotel
to ask 'em to hush down a mite."

"Hell, that's what I sent 'em outside for, so's I could
nap a little bit." The barkeep grinned. "Nights like this,
when the evening crowd starts to scatter, I like to lean
back in a chair and snatch a few winks till business
picks up in the morning. And once they get to yattering
about gunfighters like Wild Bill Longley, there ain't no
shutting 'em up."

"It's funny." Longarm frowned. "I don't have no rec-
ollection of Longley doing much around here."

"Excepting that he was born not too far from here and
killed his first men pretty close by," the barkeep replied.
"And I guess there's still some Longley kinfolks farming
over by Nacadoches and thereabouts."

"That'd make sense," Longarm said. "Whether they're
close kinfolks or not, people have got a way of remembering their relations."

"More specially when them relations has made a
name—don't matter much whether it's a good name
or a bad one."

"Well, be that as it may," Longarm said, "I guess
them men up along the bar's got their whooping and
hollering outa their craws by now, so I'm going to go

24

back to the hotel and see if I can finish out my sleep. Thanks for the drink. It was just about what I needed to finish off the day."

Back in the hotel room, Longarm closed the door, being very careful to move silently in case Lisa had dropped off to sleep during his absence. The lamp had been turned up low so that only the faint ghost of a flame flickered along the thin strip of wick, and all that he could see was the outline of her form in the bed.

After draping his gunbelt over the back of the chair beside the bed, Longarm levered out of his boots and kicked his trousers free, then slid his arms out of his shirt. He was bracing himself on the mattress with one arm, just beginning to lower himself carefully onto the bed, trying not to disturb Lisa, when she threw back the covers and sat up.

"I thought you were never coming back!" she said.

Reaching up, Lisa grasped his arm and pulled him down to the bed. Longarm landed half on the mattress and half on top of her. She let herself fall backward and carried him with her. They landed in a half tangle with Longarm's chest pressing firmly against her full-budded breasts.

"I hope you're not too tired," she whispered. "Because there's still a lot of night ahead, and if you feel like I do right now, we can start this very minute to make the most of it!"

Chapter 3

Half-asleep in his saddle after the better part of a day spent in steady travel, Longarm topped the long gentle upslope and reined in to look at the terrain. Ahead of him the road stretched in a string-straight line across a decline from the low rounded crest where he now sat his horse to the more level land in the distance. On the western horizon the glow of sunset was already beginning to tinge the sky, and he realized that he'd never be able to cover the miles that remained between Austin and his present location before darkness settled in.

Longarm had no regret for the late start he'd made. After a late-morning ham-and-eggs-and-biscuit breakfast with Lisa at the small narrow cafe, the only eating place Walburg boasted, he'd spent a good part of the morning helping Lisa rearrange the load in her wagon. After that he'd ridden alongside her for a half mile or so to make sure that the mended axle was going to perform its job.

Though he'd stayed with Lisa's wagon for only a short distance, the cool part of the morning had passed before Longarm left her behind.

Through the long day that was now coming to a close he'd passed only two solitary travelers heading east, and no towns other than three or four small huddles of houses around a trail junction. Since mid-afternoon none of these had offered any kind of travelers' accommodations, and he'd pushed ahead in the hope that before nightfall he'd find some kind of shelter with a roof over it and a bed for the night, as well as a modest restaurant where he could get a hot meal before darkness.

Sure now that there was no hope of finding any sort of shelter and food along the stretch of road that lay in front of him, Longarm resigned himself to saddlebag rations in a dry camp and a night with only blankets between him and the hard sunbaked ground. He toed his horse ahead and let the animal set its own gait as it started down the long incline.

He'd covered the better part of two or three miles, and the steadily setting sun was beginning to creep under his hat brim and flood his face with its rays, when he reached the drop-off that had been invisible from the top of the grade. The abruptly descending ground did not drop from a high ledge, but the long dusty zigzag path leading to the sun-reddened horizon was steep enough to cause Longarm to twitch the reins of his horse and slow the animal's pace as it started down.

At the bottom of the declivity Longarm reined in to give the animal a short breather. On either side of the trail ahead the brush stood head-high. Sparse as the bushes were, they grew thickly enough to have concealed the

28

man who suddenly stepped from the brush stand with a leveled rifle.

"Just hold your nag where it is, mister!" he called. "Official police business!"

As he spoke the man was pulling aside the lapel of the ankle-length coat he had on. Longarm got a fleeting glimpse of a shining silvery badge before the other man dropped his hand and let the coat fall back in place. Keeping the reins tight, he waited for the man with the rifle to add to his announcement. When the rifle-wielder neither lowered the threatening weapon nor explained the reason for his command, Longarm's caution and curiosity were both aroused.

"I don't reckon you'd mind telling me what this is all about?" he asked.

"Not a bit, stranger," the man holding the rifle replied. "Matter of fact, I was just getting around to that. First off, I better tell you that you showed good sense when you stopped. If you hadn't, I'd've shot you."

"Seems to me that's more'n the law oughta allow, even here in Texas," Longarm said. "It's what a man might do was he a bandit or an outlaw."

"Maybe it might seem a little bit outa line, but that's what we got orders to do," the still-unidentified man replied. It was clear from his tone that he wasn't pleased by Longarm's comment as he went on. "But if it'll ease your mind, I ain't no outlaw nor bandit out after your money. As a matter of fact, I'm watching this road for an outlaw right now, because we got a tip he was traveling over it. My name's Jason Philby, Texas State Police."

As much by instinct as design Longarm froze his facial muscles to keep from showing his surprise. He was familiar enough with the history of Texas lawmen to know that the unruly, graft-ridden, and almost totally corrupt Texas State Police force had been abolished with the end of the Reconstruction period. By that time its character and conduct had become an open scandal among law-enforcers across the nation.

He'd recognized at once the false notes in both the man's actions and his voice. After so many years of danger-filled encounters with ruthless, lawless men and women, his instincts told him to listen well and proceed with caution while he probed into the reasons for the stranger's unlikely statement. He decided to play the part of an ignorant traveling cowboy while he probed a bit deeper, but to proceed with care.

"Now, you got me all wrong, Officer Philby," Longarm said. "Far as I know, I ain't done a thing that'd get the law out after me."

"Well, we sure ain't after innocent people," Philby replied. "Now, the fact of the matter is, we got word from one of our friends about an outlaw that's wanted real bad. He goes by the name of Wild Bill Longley, and he's been on the run for a long time. We got a tip that he'd be traveling along this way, and we got men scattered out along all the roads hereabouts trying to nab him."

An alarm bell sounded in Longarm's mind. Hearing the name of any dead outlaw twice in the same locality was too unusual to overlook. His curiosity aroused, Longarm decided to give Philby as much rope as possible and see where the odd coincidence might lead him.

"Just in case you might be wondering, my name ain't on nobody's wanted list," Longarm protested. Playing his hand as it was dealt he continued, "It's Custis. If I had any idea the law was after me, I'd sure give a pretty to know what for."

"Well, Longley's not the only name on our wanted list," Philby went on. "To tell you the truth, we've got the names of so many outlaws in Texas on it right now that it gets to be a job sometimes to keep all of 'em straight," Philby replied. He was lowering his rifle muzzle as he spoke. "But I can tell now that you ain't the man we're after. He'd be a lot older than you, and if you'd been him, we wouldn't be talking like this right now. He'd've pulled his gun and throwed down on me. We'd be shooting by now if you was him."

"I guess that figures," Longarm agreed. Every word that Philby spoke deepened Longarm's resolution to get enough evidence on the imposter to put him behind bars. He'd learned by experience in his beginning days as a U.S. marshal that giving a suspect a seemingly free rein often resulted in the criminal unwittingly providing the evidence needed against him. He went on. "And as long as you're satisfied that I ain't the fellow you're after, I'll just go on about my business."

"If you ain't out to break the law, I'd be the last man in the world to stop you."

"That's about how I'd taken it," Longarm said. "And I hope you won't think I'm being unfriendly when I say I got to be moving along. I got a long stretch of ground to go over, and setting here won't get me to where I'm heading."

Before Longarm could toe his horse ahead, Philby spoke again. "I ain't much on giving advice, but I better tell you what I'm thinking right now."

"What's that?"

"It ain't exactly what I'd call safe for a man by hisself to be traveling after dark in that stretch of country you're figuring to cross up ahead, not while that outlaw's still on the loose. We got men strung out all over the roads between here and Austin, and not all of them are as careful as I try to be."

"Meaning what?" Longarm frowned.

"Meaning when I see a lone traveler that might be this Longley we're after, I ask questions first, like I done with you. Some of the other men on the force don't bother to ask. They just start shooting."

"Without intending no offense, Philby, I'd say that's a hell of a way for any man wearing a badge to act."

"Oh, I got to agree with you," the Texas State policeman said. "But the fact of things is what they do."

"Well, have you got any ideas about another road you can steer me to? One I can travel to in the dark that'll get me to Austin without one of your friends taking a potshot at me?"

Philby thought for a moment, then shook his head. "There ain't one I know about that you can travel in the dark when you can't see some landmarks to go by. I'd hate to think about getting blamed if you was to wind up at someplace where you don't want to be."

"I wouldn't cotton to that myself," Longarm agreed.

"What I'd say's the best thing you can do is stop right here, Custis," Philby went on. "My camp's just a few steps back in the brush, where there's a freshwater spring in a little clearing. There's plenty of room for you to spread your blankets and bunk down alongside of me, if you've got a mind to."

"Well, now," Longarm replied. His face relaxed from the thoughtful frown it had worn. "When I think on it, I'd say that's a pretty good idea. I'll just take you up on your proposition."

"We ain't got far to go," Philby went on. "But we'll

be shoving through some brush tangles and a little clump of huisache trees to get to it. It'll be easier if you lead your nag instead of trying to ride."

"You know the lay of the land here better'n I do," Longarm said. He was swinging out of his saddle as he spoke. "Go on ahead, I'll be right behind you."

Philby turned and began pushing through the undergrowth. Longarm followed him. He tried to keep up with Philby's pace, but was hampered by the livery horse. It was obviously not accustomed to any terrain that had no roads, and was bothered by the occasional branch which slapped into its face as Longarm pushed through the thick underbrush that lined the road.

After a few steps Longarm lost sight of Philby, but was able to follow him by the swishing and crackling of the densely growing bushes. After a few minutes of his slow but steady progress, the bush thinned and he saw Philby standing looking back over his shoulder. Longarm broke through the final few steps of the thinning brush and stopped a few paces away from the Texas State policeman while he took stock of his changed surroundings.

"We ain't quite there yet," Philby said. "But unless you keep in sight of me you'd likely get mixed up in this brush, so I figured I better wait up for you."

"Thanks," Longarm said. "I'll stay closer to you from here on."

"We just got a little ways left to go. I'll move a bit slower."

After they'd covered another dozen or so yards, Longarm could hear the faint tinkling of rushing water even above the noise the pair made. Then the brush line ended abruptly and gave way to a narrow strip of grassy meadow that lined the banks of a small chuckling creek. Philby stood waiting at the edge of the open strip, and Longarm halted beside him.

For a moment Longarm said nothing, but stood surveying the new vista which lay ahead. The banks of the little stream cut through the clearing, and a few paces upstream he saw the coals and ashes of a camp fire. Some broken limbs of dried trees were piled in a little heap beside the burned area. Away from the coals the ground was strewn with a litter of gunnysacks topped by a cooking-pot and skillet.

Beyond the fire ash a rope stretched between two sturdy saplings supported a tarpaulin staked along each side to form a makeshift tent. In its shelter a crumpled bedroll was half visible. In a small grassed clearing a few paces past the improvised tent a horse and pack mule were tethered, grazing lazily.

"Looks like to me that you figure on watching the road back yonder for quite a while," Longarm commented. "And I'd say you been here a pretty good spell already and aim to stay a while longer, even if it ain't as comfortable as it might be."

"Wherever I get sent to don't bother me a mite," Philby responded. "It's a job I'm getting paid to do, so it don't make much never-mind how long I stay on lookout."

"And you're the only one that's on the lookout job hereabouts?"

"You ain't seen nobody else around, have you?"

"Nary a soul," Longarm agreed. "But if that Longley fellow you're after was to pass by on that road we just left, it'd seem like to me that you'd have a partner to stand night watch."

After a moment's hesitation Philby said slowly, "Sure. I know I oughta have somebody with me, but the fact of

34

the matter is that when we go out on a job like this one we just ain't got enough men for any of us to have a partner. Texas is a pretty big place, you know."

"I found that out a long time ago," Longarm said. "I ain't seen all of it by a long shot, but I know that in Texas a man can ride far enough to meet hisself coming back."

He and Philby had kept moving while they were talking, and by now they'd reached the little clutter of the camp.

Philby gestured toward the animals as he told Longarm, "I guess the best place for you to put your nag is over yonder past where I got mine tethered. After supper, I'll have to move mine a little ways further along, to where they'll have fresh graze, so leave some room. While you're taking care of your critter, I'll get us some supper started."

"I wish I had something to throw in the pot along with whatever grub you got," Longarm said. "But I reckon you know that when a man's trying to move fast, he travels light. So I've just got to ask you for a few bites of whatever you was figuring on for supper, and pass on the favor to the first fellow I run into that's traveling light and run outa vittles."

"You do that, Custis. And don't worry about supper, I got plenty for both of us," Philby said. A half frown was forming on his face. "You know, I'm starting to get a sorta idea. I ain't figured out all the whys and wherefores yet, but I reckon I will by the time we've finished supper. Soon as we've et, maybe the two of us can have a little talk."

"Sure," Longarm agreed. "Talking's about all there is to do in a place like this. Now, I better go get my nag tethered for the night."

35

Longarm wasted little time. He let the horse drink its fill from the stream, then led the animal away from Philby's campsite to a small break in the trees, where there was a good stand of grass. He removed his saddle-bags and the animal's saddle. As he'd often done before, he improvised a tether by fastening the reins together and looping one end around the horse's neck, then tying the other end to a small but sturdy sapling.

Grass was plentiful in the little glade, and the horse had begun to graze by the time Longarm started back to the camp fire which his companion had lit. A soot-blackened skillet rested on the ground beside Philby, who was hunkered down beside an outspread grub sack. He was slicing bacon into it from what was left of a quarter-side. Several small potatoes lay on the sack beside the bacon piece.

"You need some help?" Longarm asked as he stopped beside the grub sack.

"If you don't mind doing a little bit of plate-washing, you can take them two pie pans laying over yonder and step down to the creek and wash 'em," Philby replied. "They ain't really dirty, just got a few grease spots left in 'em. Take a little dab of sand outa the creek bed to rub 'em out with. That'll get 'em clean without much trouble."

"Sure," Longarm agreed. "And I'll be right glad to peel them spuds when I get that done."

"Don't bother. I'll just slice 'em thin and drop 'em in the pan when the bacon juice starts to sizzle out. Them little thin skins just curls off while the spuds cook."

"Sounds fine," Longarm said. "And I don't mind say-ing I'm hungry. All I had since breakfast was a bite or two of jerky, and I chewed on that while I was riding."

36

"It'll be ready pretty quick," Philby promised. "And I reckon I ain't very far behind you in being hungry. Then when we finish eating, we'll have that little talk I spoke about."

Although Longarm made short work of his dish-washing chore, the potatoes and bacon were ready to be turned out of the skillet by the time he returned from the creek with the dripping plates. Philby divided the bacon and potato slices with scrupulous care, making sure the portions on each plate were of the same size.

During the short time required to dispose of their Spartan meal the two men were silent. When the last shreds of bacon and the final dabs of potatoes had been chewed and swallowed, Longarm took out one of his thin cigars and flicked his iron-hard thumbnail across a match head. He puffed the tip of the cheroot until it glowed, and then flicked away the match. After his cigar was drawing well, he turned to his companion.

"I ain't seen you light up since we got acquainted, so I don't guess you'd have much use for one of these," he said as he took the cigar from his lips.

"I never did take up smoking," Philby replied. "After a while I'll dip up a snootful of snuff, though. It's too bad I've run plumb outa coffee. About now a cup'd go down just right."

"It would at that," Longarm agreed. "But since there ain't none, I guess we might as well have that little talk you said we needed to have."

"I was thinking that myself," Philby said. He was looking at Longarm as he spoke, his brow wrinkling thoughtfully. A moment of silence passed, then he went on. "You know, Custis, I been watching you pretty close."

"So I've noticed." Longarm's voice was flat and non-committal. "You find something wrong with me?"

"Not a bit of it. In fact, it's the other way around. I keep thinking you're wasting your time cowboying—I guess that's what you do, even if you ain't told me so. You've got the look of a good top hand."

"Now, I take that as a compliment," Longarm replied.

"Well, a good cowhand can do a lot of things besides chousing steers," Philby went on. "And I guess you handle a gun pretty good too. I'd take it you've used that Colt of yours a time or two?"

"You'd take it rightly," Longarm answered. "Not that I'd like to be bragging to the sorta policeman like you are."

"I guess I can see that," Philby said. "And it does you a lot of credit." He was silent for a moment. "Now, what you said about me needing a partner when I'm after a gunman bad as this Longley fellow made a lot of sense. And I'll tell you right off that there's a big chunk of reward money that'll go to whoever brings him in, dead or alive."

"I'd guess that a big reward would make a man look for him all the harder," Longarm said.

"You can just bet it would," Philby agreed. "A big enough reward so that whoever got it—or even got half of it—wouldn't have to worry for a long time where his next meal was coming from. Now, here's what I want to ask you. How'd you like to partner up with me while I go on looking for him?"

"You mean to be a lawman?" Longarm asked. He tried to put an expression of amazed innocence into his voice.

"That's exactly what I'm talking about."

Longarm sat silently for a moment or two, then in the same innocent voice he said, "I don't know that I got what it takes to do that. Besides, wouldn't I be getting myself into trouble with the law if I made out to be something I wasn't?"

"Not if I swear you in as my deputy."

"You mean a real honest-to-goodness lawman, with a badge of my own and all like that?"

"You hit it the first grab, Custis. With a good chunk of cash as your share when we run this Longley fellow down. And the reward's going to be paid if we bring him in dead or alive."

"I reckon I'd have to do some thinking about that," Longarm frowned. "I—well, I've seen gunfights and I ain't sure—"

"Don't go getting nervous too fast, now," Philby broke in. "I'll tell you what. You sleep on it tonight and we'll talk about it some more in the morning."

Longarm did not reply at once, then he nodded slowly and said, "All right. I'll just do that. And I don't mind telling you, the more I think about it now, the better I cotton to the idea. But I guess I'm a mite too tired and sleepy right now to talk much more. Let's see how I feel in the morning."

Chapter 4

Standing a few feet distant from the dying bed of coals, Longarm glanced at Philby's makeshift tent. He swore silently but fervently for a moment when he realized that he'd left his bedroll in Lisa's wagon when they'd parted at Walburg. He considered stepping over to Philby, who had already snuggled down in his blankets for the night, and asking if he could share the shelter. He even took a half step toward the tent before his anger at his own mistake dissipated and he decided to rough out the night.

His decision made, Longarm began the job of attempting to cobble together a makeshift bed. He wrapped the saddle blanket around his chest and hips, but it was a bit too small to allow the edges to overlap and stay closed. It was also too short to cover his legs completely, and the night air was beginning to take on a warning chill. The increasingly penetrating breeze was a warning that during the coldest hours of darkness he'd need cover of some sort if he expected to get any sleep.

He tried taking his boots off and wrapping the saddle pad around his legs and feet, but the pad had not been made for such an arrangement. It was too thick to be folded and tucked, and any small move that Longarm made caused the pad to unfold and allow the cool night breeze to chill his feet. Finally, he shoved his feet into his boots again and wrapped the pad around his thighs and knees.

Before stretching out and trying to cover himself fully for protection against the light chilling breeze that was wafting across the camp from the direction of the little creek, Longarm had taken off his gunbelt and wrapped it around his holstered Colt. He tucked the unwieldy bundle into his hat to use for a pillow, but when he tried to rest his head on the hat, the thick felt squashed yieldingly and his cheek and ear bumped irritatingly against the hard steel contours of the revolver.

After he'd pushed the hat and his revolver down his side within easy reach of his gun hand, Longarm turned and tossed restlessly for a few moments while his eyes blinked into the darkness. At last his muscles stopped protesting as they adapted themselves to the makeshift bed. Longarm settled down, lying on his side in order to see the blanketed form of Philby, who was apparently sleeping soundly. He lay very still, being careful not to move in any way that would disturb the precarious comfort he'd managed to find.

"You got nobody but your own fool self to blame for this mess-up, old son," Longarm told himself silently as he finally discovered the least uncomfortable position.

"But it don't make much never-mind. You got to sleep with one eye open anyways, just in case that crooked policeman decides to make some kinda move during the night."

Half-comfortable at last, Longarm lay motionless for a few moments before sighing deeply as his drowsiness increased. He observed the last few coals of the supper fire losing their ruddy color bit by bit, until the only light in the grassy clearing came from the stars. After a few minutes of watchfulness, Longarm's pretense of sleep became a reality and in spite of his intention to stay awake and alert, he dozed.

How long he'd slept Longarm did not know. Darkness still enveloped the western sky, but tinges of predawn gray were invading the shadows in the east. Within the little glade the silence remained unbroken, but he was sure that he'd been aroused by something other than the chill which now plagued his feet.

By this time he was fully awake and remembering the need to remain motionless if he expected to retain the small amount of comfort he still had after a long and broken night. His eyes were wide open, his senses alert. He was reaching for a cigar, his hand moving by force of habit to his vest pocket, when he saw Philby move to prop himself up on an elbow.

Being careful not to move, Longarm kept his eyes fixed on the heap of bedding on the opposite side of the fire pit. By this time the final faint blush of color had faded from the few coals that had remained alive when he'd settled in for the night. Longarm did not stir even when he saw Philby sit up in his bedroll and peer at him across the black blob on the lighter-hued earth

43

that marked the location of the dead fire.

After lowering himself back to a prone position on his bedroll, Philby did not move again for several minutes. Longarm continued his covert watch. His eyes had now adjusted to the steadily brightening darkness, but in spite of the improvement in his vision, he could see his companion only as an elongated shadow against the yellowish brown soil.

At last Philby again sat up in his bedroll. Against the deep shadow of the brush that formed the boundary of the clearing, Longarm could see his face as a grayish ghostly oval, but he still sensed rather than saw the self-styled policeman's beginning movements.

Slowly and silently Philby rose to his feet. Longarm could make out his companion's form a bit more clearly now, and there was no mistaking the movement of Philby's arm as he drew his revolver from its hip holster. For a moment the policeman did not move; then he began a careful advance toward the bedroll where Longarm lay watching.

Experience and instinct began guiding Longarm's careful moves. His Colt lay beside him, still in its holster inside his crumpled hat. He brought his arm up slowly until his hand could close on the weapon's butt. His arm and fingers moving with slow and silent caution, he slipped the revolver out of its holster. Inch by inch he slid the weapon along his side until it reached chest level. He brought the Colt to a halt there, its butt now gripped firmly, his forefinger resting lightly on its trigger.

By this time Philby had reached a point directly opposite Longarm. Only the small irregular circle of coals left by the dead camp fire separated them. Without taking his eyes off Longarm, Philby brought up his weapon slowly,

44

his head canted to one side as he bent forward to get his eyes level with the revolver's sights.

Longarm did not have the amount of time Philby spent in taking careful aim, nor did he need it at such close range. He tilted his Colt's muzzle and at the same time swiveled its barrel. His shot broke the night's silence only a fraction of a second before Philby closed his finger on the trigger of his own weapon, but that was time enough.

Longarm's Colt barked its message just as the would-be murderer's finger tensed on the trigger of his own weapon, but that advantage was all that was required to ensure his survival. Philby's shot echoed Longarm's, but even while the policeman's trigger finger was tightening, the slug from Longarm's Colt slammed into his chest.

Mushrooming as it tore its way through flesh and bone, the impact of the soft lead bullet spun Philby half around as its soft lead tip expanded while plowing through flesh and rib bones into his heart. The bullet which the dying man had intended for Longarm thunked harmlessly into the soil beyond Longarm's makeshift bed, but the man who'd fired it did not hear the sound it made.

Philby was already dead, his knees sagging as he twisted in a half-spin that ended when they touched the ground. The momentum of his turn spun his limp form sidewise and backward and brought the dead man to the ground in a lurching, ungainly sprawl. His revolver dropped to the ground with a thud. Then silence again settled over the little clearing.

For a moment after the echoes of the two shots died away Longarm did not move. He then stood up stone-faced, gazing at Philby's sprawled body, then lowered his gun hand and let the weapon dangle at his side. From habit, he tried to replace the gun in its holster, but realized belatedly that he'd left the weapon's holster and belt on the ground.

He picked up the belt and buckled it around his waist, and thumbed a fresh cartridge from its loop. Swinging out the cylinder of the Colt, he removed the fired case and inserted a fresh round, then restored the weapon to its holster. He'd learned that even in a deserted place as distant from the road as was the campsite, gunfire attracted almost anyone who heard it.

Keeping his ears alert, Longarm stepped up to Philby's body and spread over it the blanket which the dead man had used for cover. Then he returned to his own makeshift bedroll and after a few moments of clumsy struggling, managed to arrange his covers as they'd been before defeating Philby's effort to kill him.

Though the small careful movements he made sounded loud in his own ears, Longarm knew that they could not be heard beyond the little glade. He was equally sure that if anyone had been passing on the road and come to investigate the shooting, he would have heard them by this time. Banishing thoughts of the few moments just passed, Longarm closed his eyes and in a short time was asleep once more.

Standing beside the small heap of fresh dirt that he'd just finished piling over the dying coals of his breakfast fire, Longarm looked at the sky.

"Old son," he muttered into the quiet sunrise air, "you got yourself into this mess, even if it did all begin while you was just trying to be nice and helpful to a bad-treated lady. Now you better figure a way to shoehorn out of it quick as you can and get back to your real job. You done what you was sent to do, and a lot more besides, but it's still going to take some time for you to get to where you can catch a train for Denver, and if you don't move fast, Billy Vail ain't going to like it."

After checking the bundle he'd made of Philby's belongings and lashing it to the dead man's saddle along with Philby's body, Longarm forked his livery horse and toed the animal ahead. The dead man's horse followed docilely enough on its short lead rope. At the road Longarm stopped for a moment to survey the winding strip of rutted, hoof-marked gravelly soil. When he saw nothing moving either to his right or left, he reined the horse in the direction he'd been taking before his encounter with Philby.

The sun was up now, its rays warming Longarm's back. He made steady progress, but there was a sameness about the road and the countryside through which it wound that somehow made the way seem longer. Only twice during the long morning did he see a farmhouse, and on both occasions it was easy to tell even from a distance that the houses were abandoned.

High noon was near when Longarm glimpsed the third building he'd seen. For the past eight or ten miles his stomach had been reminding him that the few quick bites of long-stale bread he'd managed to rustle out of Philby's tent and called breakfast had been a stopgap, not a real meal.

As he drew closer to the isolated building, Longarm could see a hitch rail stretching in front of its narrow porch and a sign over the veranda. He exhaled a deep sigh of relief when he was near enough to read the sign: "Meigs General Store." He reached the hitch rail and dismounted, decided that the led horse did not need to

47

be tethered separately, and tossed his horse's reins over the rail. Then he went inside. An elderly man, rawboned, wearing faded bib overalls and an even more faded blue shirt, came through a door behind the counter and nodded.

"Morning, stranger," he said. "Glad to see you. What might you be wanting today?"

"Just about anything I can chew up and swallow," Longarm replied. "And if it tastes good, that'll be all the better."

"Well, now. I can get you some cheese or summer sausage or both at the same time, and a hunk of fresh bread just outa Ma's oven, or soda crackers, if them's your druthers."

"Whichever's quickest and easiest," Longarm said. "Right now my belly thinks my throat's been cut, so maybe you better trot out the cheese and sausage both."

"From the way you said that, it sure sounds like you need some of everything." The storekeeper smiled as he took the chunks of cheese and sausage from the counter and started through the door. Over his shoulder he went on. "Jest settle down on that box yonder while I see to fixing you up. And if the coffee back in the kitchen ain't all been drunk, I'll bring you a cup with Ma's compliments."

"Now, that's something I'd really cotton to," Longarm said.

Following the storekeeper's advice, Longarm settled down on the wooden box. After what seemed to be an interminable time, the storekeeper returned. In one hand he carried a plate piled with heaped-up slivers of yellow cheese, sausage slices, and bread. In the other hand he held a cup of steaming coffee.

48

"You jest set right where you are," he told Longarm. "I'll put your grub on this box by you and you can dig in."

Longarm nodded in reply. He'd already helped himself to a slice of the bread and a round of sausage and was ready to bite into the bread. The storekeeper turned away, and was starting back to the counter when he paused to glance out the door. He said nothing, but continued to the counter. He stepped behind it for a moment, then swiveled to face Longarm again as he leveled the muzzle of the double-barreled shotgun he'd picked up from the corner of the wall.

"Now, you just put up your hands, mister!" he commanded. "This here gun's got buckshot in one barrel and birdshot in the other one, and I aim to pull the trigger on both of 'em if you try any tricks!"

Longarm's mouth was full of bread and sausage. He did not reply until he'd chewed and swallowed, and he was careful to keep both his hands in sight of the storekeeper. Finally he gulped the last shreds of his oversized bite.

"Don't go getting riled up," he advised the storekeeper. His voice was calm and unruffled. "There's not any need for you to get upset. I carry a badge myself, and I had to shoot that fellow out there in my line of duty. Besides, I'm not real sure he was a real policeman."

"Ain't he the one that's been camping back along the road? Texas State policeman by the name of Philby?"

"That's him, all right," Longarm agreed. "My name's Long. I'm a deputy United States marshal and I shot that man to keep him from shooting me. As for him being a state policeman, I misdoubt that he is—or

49

was—but he might've been one some time past. You mind telling me what you know about him?"

"Why—not an awful lot." The storekeeper frowned. He did not lower the muzzle of the shotgun as he spoke. "He's been in here a few times to buy grub. Said he was camping a little ways up the road. Seems like there's an outlaw loose that might be traveling on it, trying to get away from the law. But before we go on talking any longer, I guess you better prove you're who you claim to be."

"Be glad to," Longarm replied. "Now, I carry my badge in my wallet. It's in my hip pocket, so I've got to reach around behind me to take it out. Just don't you go getting trigger-happy when I start reaching to get it."

"Just so you don't grab for your gun," the storekeeper promised. "But that dead man out there showed me a badge too."

"Mine's a real one," Longarm said. With his left hand he reached into his hip pocket and brought out the wallet containing his badge. Flipping it open, he held it for the storekeeper to inspect.

"You're shore right," the man agreed after he'd studied the badge carefully. "This one's the real thing. Now that dead fellow, he wasn't real quick to pull out the badge he had, and he didn't give me no more time than diddly-squat to look at it. I reckon he done you the same way?"

"Pretty much," Longarm replied. "But being a lawman myself, I tumbled to him right off when he said he was in the Texas State Police. Why, there ain't been no Texas police force for going on ten years."

"Which is something everybody ain't likely to know, most especially strangers passing by on the road. Well,

Marshal Long, I'm real glad to make your acquaintance. Mind telling me where you're heading for with that dead man?"

"Austin," Longarm replied. "I aim to leave this truck of his at Ranger headquarters, then get the first train out to Denver. That's where I'm stationed, and the sooner I get there, the better I'll like it. I don't reckon you'd know if there's a shortcut I can take from here to get to Austin?"

"Happens that I do. You just follow this road till you get to a little town called Jonah. Ask somebody to put you on the road to Pflugerville, and once you get there it ain't but a hop, skip, and jump to Austin."

"I'm mighty obliged," Longarm said. "And I can't get there any too soon to suit me."

"I'd sooner have had one of our own men catch up with that slippery renegade," Ranger Captain Reynolds told Longarm. "But Philby might've recognized one of my own Rangers, so that's why I asked Marshal Vail to send you here on special duty."

"He tumbled to me a lot quicker'n I figured he would," Longarm said. "When I seen him coming with his revolver, I knew the jig was up, so I got off the first shot."

"Things like that happen," Reynolds said. "But the big thing is that we're rid of him. I guess he was about the last—and one of the worst—of the old crooked State Police."

"Maybe he was," Longarm agreed. "And like I told you, he was a real slick talker. Why, there was a time or two when I damn near believed what he was telling me."

"I don't suppose you found anything in his saddlebags or his other truck that'd help us run down any friends

51

Philby might've had working the same swindle?"

"You know, I didn't even take time to go through his saddlebags or his big necessary bag," Longarm answered. "But now that you mention it, there might be something in 'em that'd help you or maybe even me if we run across somebody he's swindled."

"You've got a couple of hours to wait for your train to Denver," Reynolds suggested. "Suppose we both take a look at the same time?"

"Suits me fine," Longarm said. "Anything's better than cooling my heels at the depot waiting for a train to pull in."

While Longarm was speaking, Reynolds was lifting to the desk top the bag that contained Philby's belongings. When he grasped it by the bottom and emptied its contents on the desk top, a folded sheet of paper floated to the floor. Longarm bent to retrieve it, unfolding it as he stood up.

"Now, that's a funny thing," he said as he laid the sheet of paper on the desk. "This here's a wanted poster for Wild Bill Longley, and when Philby first begun trying to get me to fall for his confidence game, it was Longley he tried to use for bait."

"Why, Longley's been dead for five years or more!" the Ranger exclaimed. "How could Philby think of using a dead man for bait?"

"You know, I come real close to asking him that myself when he started talking about the reward money a man would get for bringing him in dead or alive," Longarm answered.

"But you didn't get around to asking him?"

"Not so's you'd notice. I was afraid if I did I might tip him off that I was already a jump ahead of him."

52

"I can see that," Reynolds said.

"Far as I know, Longley's the only killer that's ever been hanged twice," Longarm went on. "And there's an awful lot of folks that still talk about him."

"Longley was a bad one, all right," Reynolds said. "But I'd think anybody who's ever heard of him would know he couldn't still be alive."

"They might not," Longarm said with a frown. "You know how some folks are, they'll believe damn near anything. After Longley was strung up down in Karnes County and walked away from the hanging tree still alive, folks might think he got away when they hanged him again five years later, in Giddings."

"I guess anything's possible," Reynolds agreed. "But if we keep on talking about Longley we'll never get through this mess on the desk."

"Let's get started then," Longarm suggested. "Because there's a big pile of papers there, and I sure don't want to get all caught up going through 'em and miss my train to Denver."

Chapter 5

Breathing deeply, appreciating the cool fresh morning breeze of mile-high Denver after the hot muggy air of East Texas, Longarm stopped at the corner to let a hansom cab and a barrel-piled beer truck pass. Freshly shaven and feeling really rested after a full night's sleep in his own bed, he made his way leisurely across the brick pavement.

Pushing through the door of the Federal Building, he mounted the steps two at a time to the second floor. Three long strides took him to the door bearing the inscription "UNITED STATES MARSHAL, FIRST DISTRICT COURT OF COLORADO," and a fourth step took him inside. The door to Billy Vail's office was closed, but the young pink-cheeked clerk looked up from his desk beside the entryway and blinked.

"Marshal Long!" he exclaimed. "Where in the world have you been? Chief Marshal Vail's done nothing but pace the floor and swear because he hasn't had a report from you!"

"Well, not that it'll make Billy Vail any happier, but none of the places I been to had a post office handy so's I could buy a stamp."

"And I don't suppose you were anywhere near a telegraph line?"

Before Longarm could reply the door of Vail's office swung open and the chief marshal stepped out. He stared frowning at Longarm before saying angrily, "You mind telling me just where in hell you've been the last three weeks?"

"Why, down in Texas, of course," Longarm replied in the mildest tone he could muster. "You oughta know without asking, Billy, seeing it was you that sent me there."

"Yes, and damn it, Long, you ought've wired me to let me know you were on the way back!"

"Why, I figured I'd get here about as soon as a telegram would. And I was right, except you're just too ornery about admitting it. And maybe it ain't my place to say so, Billy, but you're the one that's always bellyaching about how much telegrams cost Uncle Sam."

"You don't have to remind me," Vail retorted. "But this morning I got a telegram from Bob Reynolds, in Austin, thanking me for sending you to give his Rangers a hand. What the devil happened in that case you were on down there?"

"Why, nothing much, except that I had to shoot Philby. I took Reynolds all the truck Philby had in camp. I figured that if I gave it to the Rangers they might get some answers to their open cases out of going through it."

"Well, then that's over and done, and your case is

closed," Vail said. He'd cooled down by this time and his voice was milder. "So come on into the office with me while I catch you up on the case you ought to have gone out on a week ago."

"Now, Billy, I been sweating in that damn hot Texas sunshine for so long I feel like I still got steam pouring outa my ears!" Longarm protested. "Can't you give me a few days here to cool off before you send me kiting away someplace else?"

Vail was crossing his office to his paper-cluttered desk, and did not reply at once. He began searching through the sheaves of reports and advisories and flimsies sent up from the telegraph room in the Federal Building basement. At last he found the one he was looking for, and scanned it quickly before returning his attention to Longarm.

"About three days after you left, I got this message from old Judge Parker over in Fort Smith," he told Longarm. "He's got another bee in his bonnet and—"

"Don't tell me, Billy. Let me guess," Longarm broke in. "When you say he's got another bee buzzing in his bonnet, what you mean is that he wants you to send me kiting off to Arkansas again. Likely he's got some special case he wants me to work. I guess that's what it'll take for him to get rid of that bee."

"I couldn't've put it better myself," Vail said. "The old fellow's got fifteen or twenty special deputy marshals there, and it seems to me they ought to take care of just about anything that comes up. It seems to me that every time when push comes to shove, you're the one he sends out a hurry-up call for."

"Well, you got to give him credit for one thing, Billy," Longarm noted. "Judge Parker's smart enough to know when his own men can't clean out the mustard pot by themselves. Besides, he keeps 'em so busy on all the little cases he gets that I guess he figures he needs help when something kind of special comes along. What kinda case is it this time?"

Vail hesitated for a moment before replying. "I don't expect you to believe this, Long, but I'll tell you just the same. I'd guess that before he traipsed over to Texas this fellow Jason Philby was doing his business in Arkansas."

"What's Philby got to do with any kind of case that Judge Parker wants me on?"

"Like I just said, I'm guessing," Vail replied. "But if Philby tried to use Longley for bait on you, he'd've done it for others too. He probably got Longley's name spread around and Judge Parker's got wind of it."

Incredulity tinging his voice, Longarm asked, "You think the judge really believes that Wild Bill Longley's still alive and on the prowl again?"

"That's the way I see it," Vail replied. "I'm guessing he's got it in his mind that all the ruckus about Wild Bill Longley is true. He wants you to run down Longley or whoever it is that's traveling under Wild Bill's name."

"You're joshing me now, ain't you, Billy?"

Vail shook his head. From the sober look on the chief marshal's face, Longarm was suddenly convinced that Vail meant exactly what he'd said. To gain time to think before replying, Longarm took out one of his long thin cigars. He flicked the head of a match across his thumbnail and lit the cheroot. He looked up to see Vail staring at him, a sober expression on his face. In the moment when their eyes met, Longarm realized that the chief marshal was totally serious.

"Billy, you and me both know Longley's dead,"

Longarm said. "If I recollect rightly, he took the hangman's drop something close to five years ago."

His face still soberly thoughtful, Vail nodded. Then he said, "I remember it the same way you do, Long, even if I don't recall the exact date. But I'm sure he was hanged for the second time at a little town in Texas, a place called Giddings. It's not likely you've ever heard of it, but it's someplace not too far east of Austin."

"East of Austin's where I just come from, Billy. But I sure didn't run across a town by that name any place I was at," Longarm said.

Vail fell silent again, his brow furrowing thoughtfully. Accustomed after so many years to his chief's ways, Longarm sat quietly, waiting for the chief marshal to sift through his thoughts. At last Vail broke the silence.

"Damn it, Long," he said, "I don't see any way at all for me to say no to Judge Parker. If he was to ask me to send you over to him to mop up the courtroom floor or anything else like that, I'd still have to tell you to go."

"Sure, I see that, Billy," Longarm said. "I guess it'd be all right for me to take a day or two getting ready?"

"Take whatever time you need," Vail told him. "Two or three days, even a week if you need that much. I'll send the judge a wire that you'll get to Fort Smith as soon as possible. That'll keep him from bothering me any more, because once he knows you're on the way he'll just settle back and wait."

"That's fair enough, Billy," Longarm agreed. "I ain't about to drag my feet none either. I'll be on my way to Fort Smith just as soon as I can."

Carrying his rifle in one hand and his necessary bag in the other, Longarm stepped off the Fort Smith ferryboat and started up the path that led up the sloping riverbank. When he reached the street level, he turned along the levee road and followed it until he could angle across the narrow strip of shanty houses to the cut-stone Federal Building which housed Judge Isaac Parker's courtroom and office.

A short distance beyond the building he could soon see the gallows which the hanging judge kept busy. No ropes now dangled from the high frame, but the pale faces which soon became visible, pressed against the cell bars of the prison behind the courthouse, told him that the "hanging judge" did not lack candidates for the executioner's noose.

Inside the courthouse, Longarm turned into the well-remembered corridor that led to the judge's office. He tapped on the frosted glass of the door pane, and the familiar voice invited him to enter.

Judge Parker was turning away from the ponderous book that lay open on his desk as Longarm opened the door. His short beard and mustache had become even grayer than they had been at the time of Longarm's visit for the last case he'd been called on to handle for the judge. However, Parker's opaque black eyes still stared piercingly when he smiled and gestured toward the chair beside his desk.

"Marshal Long," Parker said. The stern note in his voice belied his smile. "You certainly took your time in getting here."

"That ain't my fault or Billy Vail's either, Judge," Longarm replied. "I was outa the office on a case when Billy got your telegram. He gave me just one night to sleep in my own bed before I left to come here."

"Now that you are here, there's no reason to waste

time," the judge went on. "I suppose Vail told you why I asked for you to be loaned to my office?"

"He said you're worried about a dead outlaw called Wild Bill Longley. And since that's what my being here's all about, if you got a few minutes to spare me, I'd like to get you to answer a few questions."

"Go ahead," Parker invited.

"How many times has this fellow—or ghost, if you feel like calling him that—pulled a holdup close by?"

"I'm not sure," the judge answered. "He's been reported responsible for four holdups on this side of the river. I don't know about the Texas side, but I'm reasonably sure that he's been responsible for some robberies that never have been reported. How would you feel if you'd been robbed by somebody—or something—dressed in a white sheet and brandishing a revolver in your face?"

Longarm's face crinkled in one of his rare smiles as he said, "I guess I'd feel like a plain damn fool after I'd had time to think it over."

"Exactly," Parker said. "And with good reason."

"Them four stickups, I guess they were all close to Fort Smith?"

"They were all on this side of the river. And there hasn't been one reported for over a month. That gives me the idea that whoever's staging them might've moved into Texas."

"I was getting to that," Longarm noted. "Because this last case I was on over there, I had to shoot a fellow named Jason Philby. He was claiming to be a Texas State policeman, and he didn't tumble at first to me being a lawman. When I took his effects into Austin and turned 'em over to the Rangers, there was a wanted circular on Wild Bill Longley tumbled out of the lot. And this Philby fellow popped into my mind since we started talking. You reckon it might've been him?"

"How long ago was this?"

"Counting from the time I had to shoot him, it's been a mite over a week."

"It couldn't've been Philby then," Parker said, shaking his head. "The latest robbery reported was only four days ago. It was south of here, along the Louisiana border, a little place called Langley."

"Excuse me, Judge Parker," Longarm broke in. "You meant to say Longley, didn't you?"

"I meant just what I said," the judge replied tartly. "I do know the difference between an *a* and an *o*, Marshal Long."

"No offense meant," Longarm said quickly. "But I was just wondering—"

"So did I," Parker interrupted. "And I don't mind admitting that I'm not above ordering a man to investigate what you'd call a long shot. But names of towns change, and I wondered if during the course of time the town's name might've been changed."

"Sure," Longarm agreed. "I play hunches more'n I like to think about. Sometimes it pays off, sometimes it don't."

"We'll know very soon whether there's a connection," Parker went on. "My deputy's overdue now. He's been gone four days."

"Then that stickup in this Langley place was pulled after Philby was dead. Either that, or he's turned into a real live ghost and moved up in this neck of the woods. I don't reckon your man's had time to report back?"

Parker shook his head. "He's had time, but he hasn't

reported." A frown grew on the judge's face. "I'm sure you don't think I'm the sort of man who'd believe in ghosts or in this nonsense they've started to call reincarnation?"

His voice emphatic, Longarm answered quickly. "Not in my book you ain't, not by a long shot."

"Good," Parker said. "Now, let's get back to the core of this matter. I'll have to go and open court in a few minutes. First, since it was a proved fact with witnesses to back it up, we'll both agree that Wild Bill Longley survived one hanging but not a second one."

"Nobody could argue against that. So what I take these holdups to be is that some smart outlaw wrapped up in a white sheet is parading around claiming to be his ghost," Longarm said. Then a frown formed on his face as he asked, "But what'd that get him, Judge?"

Parker said slowly, "Perhaps it would get him a great deal. His masquerade would keep anyone from identifying him, for one thing. It could throw anyone he might be interested in killing off balance just long enough to give him the edge on drawing a revolver. He could walk up to his victim—one of my deputies, even you or me, for that matter—with his pistol already in his hand, hidden by the sheet."

"And a'course nobody'd know who was under it." Longarm nodded. "It's sure a new twist, all right."

"It's a long step from the holdup man who just ties a bandanna around half his face," Parker pointed out. "And I'm afraid it's something that will give other outlaws ideas. That's why I've asked Marshal Vail to send you here. I imagine your first thought was to wonder why I sent for you, when I've got a pretty good number of men at hand here. Am I right?"

"Right as rain."

"My deputies are all good men, Long," the judge went on. "They do the jobs I send them out on, but they aren't the best in the world when it comes to imagination."

"Well, I reckon I could see how that'd work out," Longarm said, a thoughtful frown forming on his face as he spoke. "If some renegade was to start spooking folks thataway, he could likely get away with almost anything. Bank holdups, stagecoach holdups, likely a lot more."

"Exactly. As I said, all my deputies are fine men. Take any of them—the Tolbert brothers, McConnell, Rusk, Bowman, Ellis, White, Copeland, and so on down the list. There's not one of those men who'd turn away from any case I sent them on. They'd die doing their jobs."

"Sure," Longarm agreed. "I've met up with most of them, and they're all top lawmen."

"I suppose you know by now that I won't tolerate any deputy who isn't," Parker said. "But their bravery won't protect them from some damned outlaw smart enough to drape a sheet over his head on a dark night and step out from behind a building or a tree and shoot one of them on sight."

Longarm nodded as he replied, "That's something that all of us who wears a badge knows could happen, Judge. But I hope it ain't happened to any of your deputies yet."

"It has," Parker replied. His voice was curt and angry now. "Once. To Sam Toland."

"You mean old Sam's dead? And a spook killed him?"

Parker nodded as he went on. "He lived long enough to tell Rusk that what he called a ghost suddenly appeared in front of him and shot him. Rusk investigated and found a

64

space between two buildings where there were footprints which showed that the killer had obviously hidden to ambush Sam."

"And that's all you know?"

"It's the only evidence my men could find. But that's not going to happen to any of the others, not if I can prevent it."

"From what you've told me so far, I take it you want me to be a sorta wild card," Longarm said. "But I can't see how I'm going to be able to keep watch on all your deputies at once."

"I don't expect you to. They're good men, Long. They're able to look out for themselves, but nobody's good enough to foresee everything a deadly enemy can do."

"Well, that stands to reason," Longarm agreed. "Except I don't rightly see how I'm going to find a place to start."

"I'm sure you will, after you've gone through all the reports and looked the ground over," Parker assured him. "All the reports I've had so far are here in this folder on my desk. Start going through them while I take care of this case I'm hearing. I plan to postpone it, so I'll be back very quickly."

While he talked the judge picked up a notebook and laid it on the table. It was fat with slips of paper that had been stuck between the pages. Before Longarm could pick up the notebook and open it Judge Parker hurried from the room, closing the door behind him.

Longarm settled down into a chair, took a cigar from his vest pocket, and clamped it between his strong yellowed teeth. He took a match from his vest pocket, but before striking it to light the stogie, he reached for the folder the judge had left for him to examine.

"Old son," Longarm muttered to himself as he riffled through the pages of the notebook, "Judge Parker sure handed you a kind of case you never run into before. You got to go out and find a man that nobody's seen the face of and don't know where he hangs out or what he's done or how you can prove it was him that broke some law you can arrest him for."

Dropping the bulging notebook into his lap, Longarm slid his fingers into his vest pocket, feeling for a match. He'd found one and scratched his iron-hard thumbnail over its head to light it. He was puffing the tip of the long thin cigar into glowing life, the notebook resting on his thighs, when the office door opened and a hulking man with a red face, scarred with the marks of past combats, stepped into the room.

"Now, just who the hell are you?" he asked, but before Longarm could reply he saw the notebook. "Snooping in the judge's private papers, are you? Well, we'll just see about that!"

Hampered as he was by the stogie in his mouth, Longarm could not reply at once. Before he had a chance to reach up and remove the cigar the newcomer had covered the distance between the door and Longarm's chair. He brought up his arms as he moved, and his hands closed like claws on Longarm's shoulders. He lifted Longarm from the chair and began shaking him, holding him suspended in midair.

"Answer me quick, damn it!" he shouted. "Or I'll give you a beating that'll close your jaws and keep 'em closed for a week!"

Chapter 6

Finding himself suspended in midair and being shaken like a limp dishcloth was a new experience for Longarm, but neither the size of his attacker nor the awkwardness of his position baffled him. He launched a kick at the crotch of the man holding him. It landed squarely on target. The man who was holding him grunted, a snort of pain mingled with anger, as his back bowed involuntarily with the painful shock brought him by Longarm's kicking boot toe.

As he felt his boot soles grating on the floor Longarm was drawing his Colt. He jammed its muzzle into his assailant's midriff and gritted out, "Now let go of me before my trigger finger starts itching! And it's going to start in about two seconds!"

Before the man could release him, the office door opened and Judge Parker came in. Though he was no match in size or age for either of the struggling men, the judge waded into the affray. His only weapon was the notebook he carried, but he used it with a skill that neither Longarm nor the man attacking him expected.

Swiveling from one to the other, the judge began slapping with his book at both combatants. Most of his blows landed on an arm or the shoulder of either Longarm or his assailant, but he did not let up until the two stopped their struggle and stepped apart.

For a moment the three men exchanged stares, then Judge Parker said, "I want an immediate explanation of this unseemly conduct! You men seem to be overlooking the fact that this is my private office and not a prize-fighting arena!"

Longarm glanced from the judge to his attacker. "You jumped me first," he said. "I guess you better lead off."

"Go ahead, Andrew," Parker said. "If Longarm is right, it's up to you to explain why you attacked him."

"Well," the man Judge Parker had addressed as Andrew said. "Well, damn it, Your Honor, I tapped on your door and walked in here and this fellow was setting there with one of your private notebooks in his lap. I asked him what he was doing, and when he didn't answer me, I jumped him."

"Is that right, Marshal Long?" Parker asked, turning to Longarm.

"It comes real close," Longarm agreed. "Except he didn't waste no time before he sailed into me. I didn't have a chance to tell him that it was you who'd give me that notebook of yours to look at."

Returning his attention to the second man, the judge asked, "Do you have anything to offer in rebuttal, Andrew?"

"I don't reckon I do, Judge," the deputy replied. "All I

seen was him going through your private papers. I didn't have no idea you'd told him it'd be all right to look. I just figured it was part of my job to stop him."

"Commendable, but a bit too hasty," Parker said. "Now, I'll expect both of you to consider this unfortunate episode forgotten. I want you two men to shake hands and forget that it ever took place. Marshal Long, this is Deputy Marshal Andrew Blaine."

Both of them trying to hide their embarrassment, Longarm and Blaine shook hands. Blaine turned to the judge.

"What I come in here for was to report to you, Judge," he said. "I got some real bad news about that Langley business."

"Good or bad, let me hear it," Parker replied. "And since Marshal Long's taking this case over, he'd better hear it at the same time. Go ahead. You can give me your written report later."

"I don't know which part of what I got to tell you is the worst," Blaine began hesitantly. "I guess it'd be that poor old Clete Barnes got killed. I reckon it's partly my fault. I didn't stick with him as close as I might've."

"Nonsense!" Parker snorted.

"Well, we separated so's we could cover more ground faster," Blaine went on. "That's why I wasn't there to stand up with him when he got shot."

"I hope you know who killed him!" Parker snapped. "Because I'll want to see that man stand up in front of me while I tell him he's going to hang!"

"It'll likely be a while before he comes up in front of you, Judge," Blaine went on. "We got to catch him first."

"You do know who he is, though?" the judge asked.

"I can't put a name to him," Blaine admitted. "And right now I don't know of anybody else that can. But he's the same one that killed Sam Toland."

"Wait a minute!" Longarm broke in. "If the killer in Langley was all wrapped up in a bed sheet, how can anybody know it was him that killed your deputy friend?"

"Because he's got a scar on his gun hand that looks just like an *L* turned sideways," Blaine answered. "At least, that's what the sheriff down in Langley told me it was what Clete had said just before he died."

"You weren't with Clete when he was killed then?" Judge Parker asked.

"No, sir," Blaine said quickly. "You see, Judge, we'd split up—"

"Never mind the small details now," the judge broke in. "But be sure you put them in your report when you make it out." Turning to Longarm, he went on. "I think you have enough to start your investigation with, Marshal Long. And I want you on that killer's trail before it has time to get cold."

"Oh, I aim to be!" Longarm answered. "Now that I got some place to start from, I sure ain't going to let it get cold."

"I didn't expect you to," Parker observed.

Longarm went on. "Soon as I get me a bite to eat, I'll be on my way. Right now I'm so hungry my belly thinks my throat's been cut." Turning to Blaine, he said, "If Judge Parker don't mind, maybe you'll come along with me. I still got some questions I'd like to ask you, and if you just rode into town, I got a hunch you might be pretty slack-bellied too."

"By all means go with Longarm," Judge Parker said

70

quickly. "I want you to give him all the help you can."

Nodding to the judge, Blaine turned to Longarm and said, "Let's get to moving then. Shad Prentice's saloon's just down the road a piece, and he sets out a good free lunch."

Neither Longarm nor Blaine had anything to say during the few moments they spent walking to the saloon. At that hour of the day the place was deserted, and to Longarm's pleased surprise, while they were filling their plates at the free lunch counter the first thing he noticed on the saloon's back-bar was a bottle of Tom Moore Maryland Rye. He pointed to the bottle when the barkeep stepped up to serve them, and waited until Blaine had indicated his preferred tipple.

"If it's all right with you," Longarm told the barkeep, "we'll just take these bottles over to that table yonder and set down a little spell while we have a quiet talk."

"Customer's always the boss in my place," the man said. "I can just as easy keep track of how many drinks you have with you over at that table there as I can if you was to stand here bellied up to the bar."

Carrying the bottles and shotglasses along with their plates, Longarm and Blaine moved to an isolated corner table. They sat down, the table between them, and said nothing until they'd eaten and had also filled and emptied their shotglasses, then refilled them for a second round. Longarm took out two of his long thin cigars and offered one to his companion, but Blaine shook his head.

"I chaw myself," he said. "But not while I'm more interested in tasting a shot of good liquor."

"I don't reckon chewing's my style," Longarm remarked between puffed veils of smoke as he lit his cigar. "But I guess it's every man to his own poison."

71

"You ever notice Judge Parker indulge?"

"Come to think of it, I never did see him smoke or chew," Longarm answered.

"That's on account of he's a snuff-dipper," Blaine confided. "He keeps a little wad down in his bottom lip, but you'd never notice it. And come to think of it, I never did see him put a dip in his mouth."

Brief and inconsequential as it had been, the exchange between Longarm and Blaine seemed to have broken the subtle barrier that had been between them. Blaine settled back in an easier posture in his chair and looked across the small round table at Longarm, a question in his eyes.

"How come the judge sent for you all the way to Denver, instead of letting us fellows that're his regulars take care of this case he's put you on?" he asked.

"You'd have to ask him that," Longarm replied. "It might be because I worked a case or two for him before he had you and all your friends to do the legwork on his cases. From what I've seen, he sure keeps you jumping."

"Oh, there's none of us minds that. And he don't favor one of us over the others, except now and then when he runs into something like this spook bandit case. It's just like him to put you on it instead of me."

"You ain't going to hold a grudge against me on account of that, are you?"

"I don't reckon it'd do any good to." Blaine smiled. "It was the judge that sent for you to come here, and I sure don't aim to get crossways of him."

"Fine," Longarm said. "Now, suppose you start out from the beginning and tell me about this killer ghost you run into down in that little place where Judge Parker sent you."

"Langley? Well, far as I could find out, there ain't a thing to connect the town with Longley. That ain't to say it might not've been called Longley one time, but it'd've been quite some years back. Anyhow, the three or four old-timers I talked to never did agree about where the name come from."

"But I reckon all of 'em had heard about Wild Bill?"

"Oh, sure. Seems like they remembered when there was some Longleys had a pretty good-sized farm not too far outa town."

"Did they say whether there's any of them left there now?"

"That was one thing everybody agreed on. None of 'em knew they whys and wherefores of it, but it seems the whole Longley bunch just up and left one day."

"I don't guess anybody knew where they moved to?"

"Some said Kansas, some was certain they went to Wyoming, and some swore they moved to Texas," Blaine replied. "But I wouldn't be too sure that any of 'em knew what the truth of the matter was. And I didn't push any of 'em hard, because what I mainly had on my mind was finding out who killed Clete Barnes."

"This Barnes fellow was one of the judge's special deputies then?"

"Oh, no. He used to be, but he got too old and stove-up. The judge pulled a string or two and got him the job of constable down at Langley. They already had a sheriff—his name's Pat Daniels, a real good man—but Clete said he wasn't about to hang up his gunbelt for good, so Judge Parker talked Pat into helping him get the constable job."

Longarm shook his head as he said, "Which he likely ought not've tried to hold down. I've run into it before."

73

Blaine nodded agreement as he said, "Judge Parker just had a bad idea this time. Except I wouldn't like for you to tell him that I said so. He'd likely bust a gusset."

"I've heard lots of stories about his temper, and run into it a time or two myself when I was working a case for him some time back," Longarm said. "But I got to give him credit for one thing. He jumps in with both feet to catch up with whoever it was done a killing and puts 'em on trial right away. Then if the jury comes back and says guilty, he sees that they're dangling by the neck before sundown."

"That's pretty much the way of it," Blaine agreed. "Well, in this case me and Pat Daniels was stumped. Damn it, Long, you been around a while. This outlaw they're after was all wrapped up in a bed sheet. How in hell do you go about finding somebody unless you know what they look like?"

"I got to put in with you on that," Longarm replied. "It's hard enough a lot of the time to find a man you're after when you know what he looks like."

"I don't reckon it's anything new for an outlaw to doll hisself up so nobody knows who he is, but neither one of us had ever run into one that draped a sheet over his head before."

"And you're sure nobody in Langley even got a look at this killer? Not even at his boots? There's been a time or two when I've found a wanted man just because I knew what kinda boots he had on."

Blaine shook his head. "I asked about that. The killer was covered up from his boot soles to his head."

"I reckon you asked about his voice too?"

"Sure. But it seems like there wasn't nobody but poor

old Clete Barnes ever heard him say anything."

Longarm nodded thoughtfully, then he asked, "Didn't you run into anybody that said how tall or short the fellow is?"

"Oh, sure. Half of 'em said he was big, higher than six feet, but the other half claimed he was short and squatty."

"How about his hands?" Longarm prodded. "He had to show 'em, if he was holding a sixgun."

"That's about the only clue. A few witnesses have identified the "L" shaped scar on his hand. But that's not much help in finding a suspect."

"Offhand, I'd say you done about the best you could," Longarm observed.

"Even if I'd done better, Judge Parker'd expect me to've done more," Blaine said bitterly. "You'd oughta know that as well as me."

"I'll grant you that Judge Parker looks for a man to do better than he can, sometimes," Longarm agreed. "And now that you've brought his name up again and it's getting on for late, I guess we'd best mosey back to the courthouse and see if he's done with that case he's trying."

Plodding silently up the slope that led to the courthouse, Longarm and Blaine could see lights in the windows of Judge Parker's courtroom even before they reached the top.

"Looks to me like the judge is taking a long time on that case he's hearing," Blaine remarked. "And there's no telling how much longer it'll go on."

"You saying 'go on' reminds me that's what I got to be doing," Longarm commented. "Between what you and Judge Parker's told me, I got everything I need to get started on this case, and the longer it takes me to get to Langley the harder it's going to be to get a straight story from them folks down there."

"I know exactly what you're talking about," Blaine smiled. "When there's a stickup or a killing, the longer the witnesses has to think back about what happened, the guns get bigger and so does the outlaw holding one."

"All that's holding me back is getting Judge Parker to give your stableman word that I can have a horse," Longarm went on.

"Well, if you're in such an all-fired hurry to get going, I can tell the stableman it's all right for him to fix you up with a nag and saddle gear." Blaine pointed to the end of the courthouse. "The stable's back yonder, just a step or two away. If it'll help you any—"

"It sure will. If the judge is still in that courtroom, it means he's going to see whatever case he's trying right on to the bitter end, and it might be midnight before he's got a minute to give me."

"Come along, then, and we'll get you fixed up."

Ten minutes later, Longarm was holding the reins of the best horse he could find in the stable Judge Parker kept for his always-busy deputies. Andy Blaine extended his hand as he said, "I hope you ain't superstitious about somebody wishing you good luck, Longarm. But I sure do hope that's all the kind you have."

"Well, thanks," Longarm said as they shook hands. "You tell the judge we talked, and let him know he won't see me till I've got whoever it turns out to be I'm after."

"Sure," Blaine nodded. "I'll be glad to pass on what you said. Chances are he won't like it, but that'll be between him and you after you get back here to Fort Smith."

"And from what you've told me, that ain't going to be real soon," Longarm said. "I got a feeling that running down this outlaw that's took up Longley's name is going to be like looking for a black cat on a dark night."

Reining in, Longarm squinted into the darkness that gloomed ahead of him and wondered again when he'd reach his destination. The cloudless night was moonless, its pitch-blackness relieved only by the canopy of stars. The faint starshine had given him enough light to assure him that he was staying on the road and he'd kept pushing steadily ahead, stopping now and then only long enough to let his horse rest.

During the earlier hours of the night he'd seen an occasional farmhouse, usually some distance off the road, its presence revealed only by the yellow lamplight shining through drawn shades from a window or two. However, for the past hour or more he'd seen no lights on either side of the road. By this time, the long busy hours of travel from Denver with the addition of his present night ride were beginning to tell on even Longarm's iron constitution. According to the way he read the stars, midnight had passed, and he still had no way of knowing how much further he'd have to travel.

He was seriously debating whether to keep pushing on or whether to cut his losses and bed down along the roadside when a glint of brightness caught his eye. It was not beside the road, but some distance from it. While Longarm was trying to decide whether to rein his tired horse onto unbeaten ground and head for the light, another gleam, further ahead than the first, broke the horizon's darkness.

"Reckon that settles it, old son," Longarm muttered

into the hushed night air. "Two lights that close together don't mean but one thing—you're bound to be pretty near where you're headed for. Just stick it out a few minutes more and maybe it won't be too long till you can stretch out in a real bed and get some sleep before it's daybreak again."

Toeing the tired horse brought little response. His mount was as weary as its rider, though except for an occasional lurching misstep on the rutted path, the animal was still holding to the pace Longarm tried to maintain. He rode on past the two glints of light that had given him such encouragement, and soon after he passed the second gleam of brightness from the window of a house far off the road, a yellow smudge of lights became visible in the distance.

Longarm reined in, more to rest his mount than to get a better look at the hopeful brightness ahead. He said into the darkness, "Looks like you finally made it to Langley, old son. Now all you got to do is find a place that's a mite more comfortable than the hard cold ground where you can stretch out and get a few hours of shut-eye."

Reluctantly, the weary horse resumed its slow plodding in response to the gentle prodding of Longarm's boot toe. With equal slowness the lights ahead separated from a general glow into individual gleams between wide patches of darkness. The outlines of buildings and houses began to show as black silhouettes against the night-blue sky.

Suddenly the road took a sudden turn. It stretched ahead as an unpaved street lined with small houses. Beyond the houses Longarm could make out the bulkier forms of a short row of business buildings. The darkness of the street was emphasized rather than diminished by the few lights that hung over the doors of a few of the stores. Near the end of the street Longarm saw the glow of a blue lantern shade which identified doctors' offices and public buildings such as a police station. He toed his trail-weary horse to a faster walk and reined it into the street.

Chapter 7

Suddenly Longarm realized that even his spring-steel muscles needed rest. It was after midnight, and even his tough-muscled frame was feeling the strain of his long ride. He could tell at a glance along the street ahead that he was in Langley's business section, and as he rode slowly through the town he scanned the scanty array of stores and small offices that lined the thoroughfare.

Most of the buildings he passed were dark and shuttered, and he looked in vain for a restaurant or a saloon. At last he saw the sign HOTEL rising above the roof of one of the larger buildings near the end of the street, where the business buildings gave way to modest homes.

More than ready to stop and crawl into bed for a badly needed night's sleep, Longarm reined up in front of the building that bore the hotel sign. Only then did he see that its windows were shuttered and on the door there was a small sign which read: "CLOSED FOR TWO WEEKS. CALL AGAIN."

Beyond the hotel the town's business section ended abruptly, giving way to small residences. Even in the darkness Longarm could see that a short distance ahead the houses were spaced further and further apart, and past the last one the bald open prairie began.

Since the road on which he'd entered Langley had intersected the town's main street, and he'd turned into the street near what seemed to be the settlement's center, Longarm reined his horse around and retraced his original path. Shortly beyond the point where he'd ridden into town, the business buildings which were scattered along the street ended at an imposing two-story brick structure. Like the other buildings he'd seen, its ground-floor windows were dark, but a faint gleam of light trickled through the windows of the upper floor and a lighted lantern hung above its door.

Bringing his horse to a halt in front of the building, Longarm saw that the big building was more solidly constructed than most of the others on the street. On both sides of the sturdy door large windows spanned almost the entire width of the walls. There was lettering on both windows, but in the fast-encroaching darkness he could not read the signs from his saddle.

Dismounting, Longarm stepped up to the building's facade. Darkness had almost taken over now, but by leaning close to the wide windows and squinting at the letters he managed to read the signs they bore.

In the first window the sign read "LANGLEY CITY HALL," in the other window the legend was "PIKE COUNTY COURTHOUSE," and beneath it there was a smaller sign: "*Sheriff Pat Daniels. If office is closed, go around corner to third house.* "

Shrugging, Longarm led his tired horse around the corner. The third house was small but well kept. It too bore a sign on the door: "*Sheriff Pat Daniels.*"

Leaving his horse to stand, Longarm stepped up onto the porch and knocked. He waited several moments, and was about to rap again when the door opened and a youngish man stepped out. He blinked sleepily while focusing his eyes on Longarm, then said, "I'm Sheriff Daniels. What's your trouble?"

"I never like to drag another lawman outa bed, but I figured it was the only way I could find out what I need to know," Longarm replied. He took out his wallet and displayed his badge as he spoke. "My name's Long, deputy United States marshal outa the Denver office, but right now I'm here on special duty with Judge Parker up in Fort Smith."

Sheriff Daniels was wide awake by now. He extended his hand as he said, "Glad to know you, Marshal Long. I'm sorry to've kept you waiting, but folks here go to bed early. What sort of problem brings you to Langley?"

"It ain't nothing that'll keep you outa bed but a minute," Longarm replied. "Later on, sometime tomorrow, I'll need to talk with you about the man that killed the town constable the other day. But right now I'm trying to find a place to sleep tonight. I just got into town and rode up and down your main street, and it looks like the only hotel you got here's closed up. I figured you could maybe steer me to a rooming house or some place that might accommodate me."

Daniels shook his head. "The hotel's closed because the man that owns it suddenly keeled over and died a week or so ago. And I know that since it's closed all three of the rooming houses here are packed full. One of them's even sleeping people in the hall. There just isn't a place in Langley right now where a stranger can rent a room for the night."

"I halfway figured you'd tell me something like that," Longarm said. "And when I figured I'd stop and have a drink, it just come to me that I didn't see a sign of a saloon."

"Langley's a temperance town, Marshal Long. As a matter of fact, the whole county's temperance. The nearest saloon is twenty miles away."

"I sorta figured that was the way of it," Longarm said. "Well, I guess I'll just have to ride on out to the prairie and find a place where I can spread my bedroll on the ground. Not that it'd be the first time."

"I'd invite you to stay here at my place, except for one thing," Daniels said. "My wife's kinfolks are in town visiting and we haven't any room at all. Their young folks are sleeping on pallets on the floor."

For a moment Longarm was silent, then he came up with the suggestion of a solution that had entered his mind. He said, "I guess you've got a jail. I ain't above sleeping on a cell bunk."

"You'd be welcome to use one, if I had it," Daniels said. "Except that the jail's about as crowded now as the rooming houses are. I arrested a bunch of strangers that set up a still and started making some pretty bad whiskey, which is against the law. And there's the usual number of tramps and petty thieves. I don't . . ." He paused, frowning, then went on. "Hold on a minute, Marshal Long. Maybe I can help you after all."

"Now, I don't mean to be a bother—" Longarm began.

"No bother at all," Daniels broke in. "I was about to say I've got a full jail because it's only got two cells, a big holdover and a little separate cell where I keep the hardcases. There's a prisoner in that small cell now, a saddle tramp who was down on his luck and turned robber. He's not a hardcase, so if you don't mind sleeping in the cell, I can put him in the big room for the night with the bums and whiskey-makers and let you have his bunk. Fresh bedding, of course."

"I'd sleep on the bare ground in hell's half-acre tonight, long as I had a mattress under me," Longarm said with a smile. "And I'd sure be mighty much obliged if you don't mind taking the trouble to fix me up."

"No trouble at all, Marshal Long. Just let me go inside long enough to step into my boots. Then we'll walk back to the jail and I'll make you just as comfortable as I can, considering the circumstances."

While waiting for Daniels to return, Longarm fished out a fresh cigar and lit it. The young sheriff came out again after a very few minutes. This time he carried a ring of jangling keys. He gestured toward the blocky building where Longarm had stopped a moment earlier.

"You'll be settled in pretty quick," he said. "And don't worry about your horse, Marshal Long. I can put it in the county stable. It's right in back of the building here. If you want to get your saddlebags you can just let him stand, and I'll take care of him after you're settled in."

"Now, that's real accommodating of you," Longarm replied as he lifted the saddlebags off the horse and tossed them over his shoulder. "We need to do some talking about this case I come here on, and sleeping in that cell is going to put me right on hand early tomorrow morning."

85

"I guess you've come down here to look into that shooting scrape when one of the town constables was killed?"

"That's the size of it," Longarm agreed. "And to make sure there ain't nothing to the talk that's going on about Wild Bill Longley coming back from the dead."

"I've gotten just a hint or two of that yarn," Daniels said. From the tone of his voice Longarm could form a mental picture of the frown that must be on his companion's face. Daniels went on. "But you must've heard rumors or gossip of that kind about other gunfighters who've made big names for themselves."

"Oh, sure. And if even half of them stories was true, there'd be enough old-time gunhands still alive to keep fellows like you and me on the jump all the time."

"I'm just as satisfied that there aren't any more like Sam Bass and Big Nose Curry and Billy McGinness and a bunch of others I could call by name. If all the old gunhands were put together in one place, there'd be enough of them to make up a pretty-good-sized army," Daniels said. "But there certainly aren't any more like Wild Bill Longley. From everything I've heard, he was about as mean as they come."

"Maybe a mite meaner," Longarm agreed. "And whoever it is passing themselves off for him is apt to be as mean as he was—leastwise that's what Judge Parker thinks. That's the reason why I'm here. You know the judge, I guess?"

"I'm sure I don't know him as well as you do, likely not as well as I ought to."

"Well, when Judge Parker gets an idea into his head, it takes something like a blast of dynamite to get it out. And the bee in his bonnet right now is that there's some sorta string that ties up old Wild Bill Longley with this town here, because it's called Langley, and that the fellow wrapped up in a bed sheet that killed your constable is working up to be a new Wild Bill Longley."

"That certainly doesn't sound like the judge to me," Daniels said. "What do you suppose gave him an idea like that?"

"It's sorta hard to figure," Longarm answered. "But you know how judges get to be sometimes. They're about the only men I know that think they got to be right all the time."

"Yes, I've noticed that," Daniels said. "Well, Marshal Long, I'll sure be glad to give you any more help I can tomorrow, but I was away on the day of that shooting."

"I don't think that makes much never-mind. Now, the story I got was that you were the first lawman here after it happened, so maybe what you heard about it while it was still fresh in everybody's mind might give me some ideas."

They were nearing the jail building by now and Daniels gestured for Longarm to halt. He said, "As it happens, I was out in the county on a case. But I got statements from the two men who got to poor old Clete after he was shot and just about dead. But in spite of what you've heard, he didn't say a word about recognizing the man who shot him. He was too far gone and he died only a minute or so afterward."

Longarm nodded as he replied, "I sorta figured it was one of them wild tales that nobody knows who it was started them. But we'll go into that shooting tomorrow, after I've had a good night's rest."

"We'll have to stop in my office for a minute," Daniels said. "I don't carry the keys to the jail when I'm out in the field. It's easier and safer to leave them in my desk drawer."

"I can see where it would be," Longarm agreed.

"I do carry my office keys, though. Including those to the back door. This building's so big and sprawled-out that it saves me a lot of time to go in the back when I'm coming here from the house. But we won't need to spend a lot of time, and we can take the inside steps going up to the jail."

"Ain't your office where you got them witness statements we was talking about a minute ago?" Longarm asked.

"Yes, of course."

"I hate to impose on a man, Sheriff," Longarm went on. "But would it be a lot of trouble to get them out and give me a chance to look 'em over real fast? It might save us both a lot of time tomorrow."

"I can see where it would," Daniels agreed. "Time's bound to be pretty important to you, and while I honestly don't think you'll get much good out of them, you might get some ideas you can be thinking 'bout tonight."

"That's pretty much what I got in mind too," Longarm said.

While they'd been talking, Longarm and the sheriff had reached the rear of the huge sprawling building. The sheriff stopped at the door and Longarm followed his example.

"We'll save a lot of walking by going in the back way," Daniels said. "It's easier than going all the way to the corner to the front door."

"You sure got a big building here for such a little town," Longarm commented. "I'd bet it cost a sight of money to put it up."

"Not as much as you might think. There was a lot of work donated, and the judge gave some of the petty prisoners a choice of going to jail or working on the building job." As he spoke, Daniels unlocked the door and opened it. He went on, "I'd better go in first. I'll strike a match right away. I always make sure there's a lamp handy back here. Those reports you wanted to look at are still in my desk drawer. I'll get them out and leave the lamp for you while I pick up my jail roster. I want to take it upstairs with me when we go."

Longarm followed Daniels into the big dark chamber, and blinked when the light of the match the sheriff struck flared in the big dark chamber. By the time Daniels had touched the match to the wick of the lamp that stood on a small table just inside the door, and the softer glow of the lamp replaced the flaring match, Longarm's vision had gotten adjusted to the light and he took the thin sheaves of paper handed him by the sheriff.

Bending over the table, he read the few brief lines which made up the statements. Witness Jonathan Small had first noticed something white in the road when he'd come out of a store down the main street. He'd quickly identified it as a man wrapped in a bed sheet and started walking toward the swathed form, when the town constable appeared on the street beyond the white figure and waved him away.

He'd heard a gunshot and seen the constable fall. While he was running toward the scene of the shooting, the sheet-wrapped man had turned to fire at him, but missed. Small had dropped to the ground when the sheet-disguised man triggered off his shot, and when he raised his head to look again, the disguised shootist was firing another shot, this one at a man approaching from another direction. Small had dropped his head and shielded his eyes, and had seen nothing more until he'd heard hoofbeats and seen the constable's body on the street and the killer riding off, still wrapped in the disguising sheet.

Putting down the thin sheaf of papers, Longarm picked up the second statement. It was signed by Pleas Randall, who'd witnessed even less than Small. All that Randall had seen was the constable's body on the ground and the fleeing killer making his getaway.

"You can see from that how much I had to go on," Daniels said as Longarm laid the thin sheaves of paper aside. "And I still don't have anything more."

"I guess you asked around to find out if anybody'd seen the killer ride into town, or got a look at him while he was wrapping up in the bed sheet?" Longarm asked.

"I think I've talked to half the people in town, trying to find somebody who'd seen that murderer ride in or gotten a look at him while he was wrapping himself up in the bed sheet," the sheriff replied. "I've questioned three or four other men who were in this general area before the—well, ghost, I guess you'd call him—showed up. Apparently nobody saw him until the shooting started."

"It does happen that way," Longarm said. "People look, but they don't see things." He stood up. "Well, thanks a lot, Sheriff. I might wanta look up them two fellows and talk to 'em, later on. Right now about all I'm interested in is getting some shut-eye. You go ahead and I'll be right behind you."

"I've got the keys to the back door of the jail," Daniels went on. "It's easier to go that way than going all the way around to the front. We'll just go up the outside steps to the back door."

As they talked, the young sheriff was leading the way to the stairway he'd mentioned. Longarm followed him up the steps, and waited while Daniels unlocked the sturdy metal door that led into the jail, flooding the landing with a glow of yellow lantern light, and gestured for Longarm to enter first.

Stepping into the narrow slit of a hall, Longarm looked at his surroundings. He and the sheriff were crowded into a short shelf-lined passageway. The shelves held blankets and pillows. At the end of the crowded entry he looked through a grillwork of bars into a small cell where a man was stretched out on a narrow bunk.

Beyond another barred partition there was a larger cell, one which took up the remaining floor space. Bunks filled three of the four walls. Most of them were unoccupied, and a majority of the half-dozen or so prisoners in the occupied bunks were sitting up, their eyes blinking after their sudden waking, squinting toward the newcomers.

"You're going to have to move in with the other prisoners for the rest of the night," Sheriff Daniels told the sleepy-eyed occupant who had risen by now to sit on the edge of his bunk in the small cell. "Step lively. The sooner you move, the quicker you can get back to sleep again."

Rising slowly to his feet, still half-asleep, the man in the small cell stumbled to the cell door. The sheriff took him by the arm, steered him to the door of the large confinement area, and ushered him inside. By this time the prisoners in the big compartment were pressing up to the barred partition, watching curiously.

"You men go back to bed," Daniels said. When they began to shuffle away from the partition, he turned to Longarm and went on. "I'm sure you've handled a lot more prisoners than I have, Marshal Long, so I won't offer you any advice about what to do if the men disturb you."

"I don't reckon I'll need any," Longarm replied. He nodded toward the lighted lamp hanging from a hook in the ceiling. "I take it you leave that light on all night?"

"Yes, of course. Is it going to bother you?"

"Feeling the way I do right now, once I get to sleep good, you can shoot off a cannon right over my head and it wouldn't bother me."

"If you're that sleepy, I don't suppose the prisoners talking to each other will bother you either."

"It might if they was close enough to yell right in my ear, but as long as they just talk, I misdoubt I'll notice. And I don't aim to bother them, unless I snore awful loud, which is something I don't generally do. I figure they'll behave all right, as long as only one of 'em's got any real serious charges against him."

"I'm sure they will," Daniels said. "I hope you get a good night's rest. I'll be here about seven o'clock, and we can talk while we're having breakfast together."

"That'll suit me just fine," Longarm nodded. "And I thank you for the trouble you've took getting me settled here. Now, I'm going to turn in. That bunk looks mighty good to me."

Chapter 8

After Daniels left to return home, Longarm stepped to the shelves of bedding and took out a blanket and pillow. Back in the cell, he cleared the bed of its old coverings and piled them in a corner. He spread the fresh blankets on the bunk's lumpy mattress and dropped the pillow at one end.

Unbuckling his gunbelt, he sat for a moment on the side of the narrow bunk before levering out of his boots. He laid the boots on their sides just below the edge of the bed and placed the holstered Colt on top of them. Longarm's thoughts were elsewhere, concentrated on the case that he was working. His moves were automatic, the results of habits formed through the years, habits that had helped him survive nighttime surprises. Longarm positioned the revolver carefully, placing it so that his hand would encounter the butt without groping or fumbling if any need arose during the night for him to reach for the weapon.

Longarm did not take off his vest, but unbuttoned it from top to bottom before tucking his backup derringer in the right-hand waistline pocket. This was another reflection of habit, but one which had on several occasions enabled him to get off the first shot when he'd been facing a night-stalking killer.

Satisfied at last, Longarm stretched out on the narrow bunk and closed his eyes. He tossed and squirmed for a moment until he'd fitted his lean muscular frame into a satisfactory adjustment with the unfamiliar bedding. Finally getting settled to his satisfaction, he was beginning to drift off into slumber when one of the prisoners broke the silence with a loud whisper that brought Longarm wide awake again.

"Hey, Lazy!" the man called. His voice had a raw hoarse edge and his effort to whisper was anything but successful.

"What's chewing at you now, Dinkey?" the man addressed as Lazy asked.

"I was wondering if you was asleep or if you was still as wide awake as I am," the one called Dinkey replied.

"Well, if I wasn't wide awake a minute ago, I sure am now. Damn it, I was just getting good asleep! What in hell kinda bee you got in your bonnet this time that's worth me waking up again to hear about?"

"I been keeping an eye on that fellow who just come in, the one that's bunked down in Jimbo's old cell. I was waiting for him to get good sound asleep," Dinkey replied. "It taken awhile, but now he's finally dropped off."

"What about him?"

"Did you hear what the sheriff called him?"

"Can't say as how I did." Lazy's soft slow drawling voice showed at least one reason why he'd acquired his nickname. "I wasn't but about halfway waked up when him and the sheriff commenced palavering."

"Well, I was awake and I heard the sheriff call him Long," Dinkey went on. "Marshal Long."

"You sure you heard right, Dink?" Lazy asked. "Because if you did, I'm going to play possum and keep my face hid till he's gone on his way. My name's still on some wanted flyers."

"He heard right, because I heard him myself," another of the prisoners put in before the man called Dinkey could reply. "Marshal Long. And there ain't but one lawman I know that's got that name. He's the big mean federal marshal that works outa Denver, the one they call Longarm."

"No question about that, Jimbo," Dinkey said. "There ain't no chance of being two of 'em. And him being here might mean Lazy and me are in real trouble. For all we know, it's us that he's come after."

"Nah," Lazy growled. "It's been too long a time since we robbed that mail train outa Denver. Everybody in that part of the country's forgot all about us, and nobody here's wise to who we are."

"I wouldn't lay a cash-money bet on it," Jimbo broke in. "I've heard about Longarm myself. They say he never has give up on any case he starts out on, and I'd sure hate to think he's come here looking for me."

"Now, if I was you, I wouldn't waste time worrying about that," Lazy said. However, his voice did not carry the positive tone that had marked it before. He went on. "You know how law officers acts when one of 'em gets shot, even if he ain't nothing more'n a town constable. They figure they got to get even. Longarm's come here to help the sheriff."

"I'd say that's the way of it, all right," Jimbo broke in. "When a lawman gets hisself killed, they don't let up on whoever it was that done the shooting. They'll stay on his trail till hell freezes over."

"That's what I'm getting at," Lazy said quickly.

"What you're saying is, you figure Longarm's here because the damn fat fool that claims he's Wild Bill Longley's boy didn't have no more brains than to go shoot that constable after the sheriff turned him outa jail the other day?" Dinkey asked.

"Maybe you can give me a better reason?" Lazy demanded.

Neither of the others spoke for a moment, then Jimbo said, "I bet you've hit on it. That's what he's here for, all right. He ain't interested in us."

"Then I feel real sorry for that fat fellow who was damn fool enough to shoot the constable," Lazy went on. "Does either one of you believe his story about being Wild Bill Longley's boy?"

"Whether Longley's his pappy or somebody else is, you put the right name to him. He's a damn fool, all right," Dinkey agreed. "I paid some attention to what he said, the first day or so he was locked up with us, but he talked too wild for me."

"I guess the sheriff figured he was a little mite touched too," Lazy volunteered. "Because he just went and turned him loose, never did haul him up in front of the judge."

"I'd sure like to know how he talked hisself into getting outa here too. If I could find out, I'd play the same game myself," Lazy said. "I know I never had as much luck getting out of a jail as he did."

"Well, I couldn't see as it was anything he done or didn't do," Dinkey observed. "Why, if that fat stuffed-up ninny was to get caught out in a gully-washer rain he wouldn't have gumption enough to take cover."

"Now you're right about something for a change," Lazy agreed. "But I sure didn't believe a word he said about being Wild Bill Longley's boy. If the real Wild Bill had been his daddy, he'd've learned him better'n to get arrested."

"He was too drunk to think about things like that when the constable brought him in. And he don't look much like his pappy did. I don't guess he's as smart either."

"If his pappy hadn't got strung up, he might've brought the boy up to be a man," Jimbo put in. "Old Wild Bill never did try to hide who he was by wrapping hisself up in a bed sheet."

"Hell, the boy had to do something like that to keep anybody from seeing how fat he is," Lazy said. "Once you seen him, you'd know him from ten miles off on a dark night."

"Well, like I said a minute ago, I got him figured for a damn liar," Lazy said. "All that foofaraw he was spouting, what a big man he aimed to be, how he come here from wherever that little place he talked about is. Giddings, he kept saying, Giddings this and Giddings that. You ever heard of it, Dinkey?"

"Oh, it's a real enough place, all right," Dinkey replied. "That's where Wild Bill Longley got took on his last necktie party. I never was there as I remember, but I might've been. I done an awful lot of moving around when I used to be friskier."

"Giddings," Jimbo repeated. "Seems to me I went through there a time or two when I was saddle-tramping around trying to be a cowhand. The way I remember it, it wasn't such a much of a town."

"Well, you can say what you want to, but I still got my doubts," Lazy told his companions. "From what I've heard about him, Wild Bill was as good with a bullwhip as he was a Colt, and he'd've laid the lash on that boy's butt real good, learning him what to do and what not to."

"There's only one thing makes me think he might've told us the truth," Jimbo said thoughtfully. "He got away scot-free because he didn't waste no time gunning down that constable who was starting for him."

"Sure. And look at what he got for it. No cash, nothing but a shooting that's got the law after him."

"But he got away!" Jimbo repeated. "Chances are he'll get off scot-free because nobody looks for a fat man to be on the wrong side of the law. Anybody that sees one fat as he is ain't likely to forget him. And the rest of us is still in here, but I guess by now he's halfway to Texas and the place where he said he was heading for, that little town called Giddings, where his daddy used to live."

"And I'd say he's got a pretty good chance to make it, the head start he's got," Dinkey observed. "And being hid by that bed sheet he had wrapped around him, nobody knows what he looks like."

"Maybe." There was doubt in Jimbo's tone as he broke in again. "But I'll still put in with Lazy. I figure the fat man's one of them damn fools that was hiding behind the door when the brains was passed out. Why, if you was to give him a boot full of water and tell him to empty it out, chances are he'd bore a hole in the sole instead of just turning it upside down."

"You might be right at that," Dinkey agreed. "But if it's all the same to you, I'd just as soon all of you'd cut out the gab and go back to sleep. I was right in the middle of a fine dream about a little redheaded gal I used to bed with up in Colorado, and I'd like to go back to sleep and finish it."

A few snickers greeted his remark, but after they'd died away the men in the big cell grew quiet. Several times during the conversation he'd been listening to, Longarm had been tempted to break off his pretense of sleep, but he'd realized that overhearing the exchange between the prisoners was worth a great deal more to him than another credit mark on his arrest record.

With their conversation ended the jail was quiet now, but in spite of feeling a bit tired at the end of his long busy day, sleep came slowly to Longarm. He turned from one side to the other several times, fitting together the bits and pieces of the remarks he'd overheard, usually pausing a moment or so to stare at the ceiling before completing his restless movement. The men in the big cell were quiet now, except for a few rasping snores and an occasional jumble of meaningless words as one or another of them muttered something unintelligible in his sleep.

Longarm stayed awake, his mind juggling his alternatives, until he was sure the prisoners in the adjoining cell were not going to resume their conversation. For a moment he considered getting up and rousing Sheriff Daniels again in order to get his horse from the stable and set out for Texas at once.

Common sense canceled his impulse after a brief

thoughtful interval. Traveling at night over unfamiliar country had often proved to him that waiting till daylight was the course of wisdom. Squirming into the most comfortable position he could find, Longarm closed his eyes, and before two minutes had ticked away he was sleeping soundly.

Though the metallic rasping noise that broke the silence of the jail was almost inaudible, Longarm was rising to sit up in the narrow bunk even before his eyes were fully open. As though guided by instinct his hand went to the butt of the derringer in his vest pocket. His fingers were closing on the compact little weapon as the door from the stairway swung open, and even in the dim gray light of the just-dawning day Longarm recognized the tall lean form of Sheriff Pat Daniels.

Releasing his grip on the derringer, Longarm swung his legs over the edge of the narrow cot and sat up as he said, "Morning, Sheriff. Ain't it a mite early for you to be coming in, seeing as how I kept you up so late last night?"

"Oh, it doesn't matter how late I go to bed. I always wake up at my regular time," Daniels replied. "And I figured that you might be hungry. Last night I didn't think to ask if you'd had any supper."

"Why, I'd've let you know if my belly'd been yelling at me," Longarm replied as he swung his feet to the floor and sat up. "Fact is, I'd already chomped down some grub outa my saddle rations before I got into town."

"But you're not going to refuse my invitation to breakfast, are you? Our relatives have already eaten and left for home. My wife's just put a fresh batch of biscuits in the oven. She's taking the bacon out of the skillet right about now and getting ready to cook the eggs."

"You make it mighty hard for a man to say no," Longarm replied. "You'll see the sky full of snowflakes on the Fourth of July before I turn down good home cooking. But it just happens I got a few little things I need to talk over with you. Just give me time to step into my boots, and I'll be ready to go along with you."

"Scotty—he's the helper at one of the boarding-houses—he'll be bringing up breakfast for the prison-ers in a few minutes," Daniels went on. "And he'll stay until they clean their plates. It seems that if he doesn't wait and take all the dishes back with him, the prisoners manage to break a few. So you see, we'll have plenty of time to talk. But I'm still not sure that I can help you a great deal."

"Right now, any help I get will be a lot," Longarm assured him. He was standing up and stamping his boots firm as he spoke. "Now I'm as ready as I'll ever be. And I played possum after I got in bed last night and heard a few things you're likely to be interested in. I'm real curious to hear what you think about what them prisoners said when they was hashing over that killing here, because it don't fit in with anything I've ever heard about Wild Bill Longley."

"I certainly don't mind telling you," Daniels said. "But let's don't get started talking about it until we've had our breakfast. I always talk better on a full belly than I do on an empty one."

"Well, I got to say that's the best breakfast I've sat down to in a long time," Longarm announced as he pushed his empty plate away and reached for his coffee cup. "When

101

your lady comes back from doing her errands, you be sure to tell her thank you for me, if I ain't still here to do it myself."

"I'll do that," Sheriff Daniels promised. "Now let's get down to this case you're looking into. Both of us know that the man who shot Clete Barnes couldn't possibly have been Wild Bill Longley."

"Oh, I tossed out that idea right off," Longarm said. "I ain't arguing about that."

"Are you as sure as I am that Longley was hanged down in a little place in Texas, a town called Giddings?"

"Sure. You and me both know that, Sheriff Daniels," Longarm agreed. "But did you ever hear about him being the daddy of a boy baby before he got caught up with?"

"Now, that is news!" Daniels exclaimed. "But are you saying that the boy grew up and turned outlaw too?"

"Well, they say boy babies takes after their daddy, and I can't think of but two reasons Wild Bill Longley'd go to a place like Giddings. One's to hide out, the other one'd be to see his lady friend and his boy, if I'm right about him having one there."

"When you put it that way, it makes sense," Daniels agreed. "And you think his boy grew up there?"

"Was I to find out that's the way of it, I wouldn't be fazed a bit," Longarm answered.

"And he was the fat fellow that got into such a little scrape that I let him go without putting him through court?"

Longarm nodded. "It seems like that's the way of it. Not that I blame you. There wasn't no way for you to know who he was, because I'd bet a silver dollar to a green apple that he was traveling under another name."

"Yes," Daniels said. "He called himself Bob Richards. And it's a name I never did see on any wanted flyers, so I played the fool and turned him loose and got a good man killed by being a careless damned fool!"

"Everybody's got to play the fool now and again," Longarm said. "I misdoubt anybody's going to hold it against you."

"Well, they should, damn it!" Daniels exclaimed. "And I've messed up your case too!"

"I'll cure that real fast," Longarm promised. "But there's more to it than I've got to yet, if I can believe what I heard when I was playing possum while some of your jailbirds was talking last night."

"Now you've really got my curiosity up," Daniels said. "Go ahead. I'm listening."

"Seems like Wild Bill's boy growed up to be a fat man. Now, can you come up with a better reason than that for him draping himself under a bed sheet to keep folks from recognizing him while he's pulling a holdup?"

Daniels did not reply for a moment, then he said slowly, "No, I don't believe I can. Can you?"

"Not if it's something a man can believe," Longarm replied. "Now, you're a lawman, Sheriff Daniels. How'd you like to be sent out to find an outlaw when you don't know where he is or what he looks like or anything else about him?"

"I wouldn't like it," Daniels replied promptly. "Unless I had some idea of what he looked like, maybe what he talked like, or who his cronies were, where he'd likely be hanging out. If I didn't know most or all of those things, chances are pretty good that I wouldn't have much luck getting on his tracks."

"That's what I've found out too," Longarm agreed.

"Then I take it you're going to Giddings?" Daniels asked.

Longarm nodded. "The shortest and the fastest way I can get there. I don't work this part of the country much, but I figure you oughta know what way that is."

Daniels was silently thoughtful for a moment before he replied, "I hate to say this so early in the morning, but the railroads haven't been very good to these parts. There's no such thing as a short way or a fast way to get there from here. The best I can suggest is for you to go back to Fort Smith and start fresh."

Longarm shook his head as he said, "I'd as soon walk into a cage with three hungry lions waiting for me as to go back there and tell Judge Parker what little bit I've done since I seen him last. He didn't have me come all the way from Denver to set out on a wild-goose chase, which is what I got a hunch I'm doing."

"Start riding west then," Daniels advised. "A good day's ride will get you to a new spur line the St. Louis & Pacific is putting in. When you show your badge, I'd say it's pretty sure they'll figure out how to put you on a train that'll get you into Texas. Once you're there I'd imagine you'll find a way to get to Giddings."

"That's what I needed to know," Longarm said. "And I do thank you for all the help you've give me. I'll stop by the stable and saddle up my horse and be on my way."

Longarm reined in at the beginning of a long stretch of gentle downslope and gazed through the glistening misty air at the huddle of houses below. Though he'd have been willing to testify in court that the East Texas rainy season had officially begun the instant he'd stepped off the work train at the railhead, he'd ridden through the spell of bad weather. The downpour was now a two-day ride behind him and the sun was beginning to do its work. Even now when he looked back at the flat line of the northern horizon, the gray clouds stretching far to the southwest were starting to dissolve as the sun's heat reached them.

At almost the exact midpoint between north and south the level horizon, elsewhere along its length as straight as a taut string, was broken by the barely visible roofs of a small town. Longarm did not need to consult his map. Since he'd followed the directions given him by the railhead crews, he was pretty sure that the town which still lay a full day's ride ahead was Giddings.

Pausing only long enough to fish a cigar from his vest pocket and light it, Longarm toed his horse back into motion and started toward the barely visible buildings of the town.

Chapter 9

Now that he could see the ragged line of rooftops breaking the horizon ahead, Longarm relaxed in his saddle. For the first time since he'd begun following the somewhat vague directions given him by the work-crew foreman at the end of track construction camp, he felt completely sure that he was now within what he called "spitting distance" of Giddings, the town which was his objective.

In the slowly deepening twilight all that he could see of the town at the moment was the line of rooftops straggling across the virtually straight horizon. Only a glance was needed to see that very soon even the line of mottled gray where sky and earth came together would be swallowed by darkness.

When he began thinking back and totaling up in his mind the number of hours he'd been in the saddle of his tiring horse, Longarm realized that the foreman of the track crew had been a good deal less than accurate in estimating the town's distance from the end of the new railroad line. Studying the terrain, he also realized that he'd be doing well to reach his destination in the short time left before nightfall took over the land.

Longarm was accustomed to the illusion of a long-lasting sunset which fooled so many newcomers, an illusion created by the thin clear air of the sparsely settled country through which he was traveling. Though the temptation to move faster was great, he did not intend to try pushing ahead too fast and perhaps crippling his tiring horse.

"Old son," Longarm told himself as he slipped one of his long thin cheroots from his vest pocket and flicked a match into flame with his thumbnail, "it seems like damn near everybody you talk to in Texas feels like they've got to complain about how crowded it's getting these days, but so far you ain't seen nothing to prove they're right."

Four days had passed since Longarm had set out from the rail-end work camp of the track-laying crew where he'd used his badge to requisition a horse and provisions. During those four days he had not made the mistake of trying to move too far too fast. He'd let his horse set its own gait across what in many places had once been fertile farmland, and was now semi-arid wasteland marked only by the tumbledown remains of what had once been houses and barns and stock fences. By the end of the second day he'd understood the meaning of the dreaded word *drought*.

Though at the moment his mount showed no signs of tiring, even after it had covered the long stretch from the last trickle of water in what had once been the bed of a rushing river, Longarm judged that the animal had finished the ten miles or so he allowed himself to cover without resting when he was on a long ride. As anxious as he was to reach his destination now that it was so close, he reined in to let the horse rest while he dismounted and paced back and forth for several minutes.

At this stop he did not prolong the rest period for his mount or for his own leg-stretching. Darkness was too near, and he wanted to get at least a glimpse of Giddings while he could get a good look at the town and its surroundings. Now all that remained of daylight was a thin bright thread between the obscurity of the land and the steadily darkening western sky.

"You still ain't going to make it before dark, old son," Longarm told himself aloud. "But right now ain't the time to try moving faster, even if chances are that whatever kinda bed you find ain't going to be a lot more comfortable than a bedroll on this damn hard prairie dirt. But the good thing to think on is that there'll likely be a place where you can buy a drink and set down to a plate of grub that you didn't have to wrestle up yourself."

While Longarm had been pacing to get the kinks out of his own legs, the last rays of sunlight had dwindled and finally vanished, giving way to the oncoming deep blue of nightfall which now tinged the darkening eastern sky.

Widely scattered gleams of light were already showing from the town ahead, aimless straggling zigzags darting through the deepening gloom, and a puzzled frown grew on Longarm's face as he realized there was no rhyme nor reason to their location. He was accustomed to riding toward towns in the darkness, but the lights in most of the settlements he'd approached had been spaced in squares or rectangles.

As he drew closer he saw the reason for lack of order in the sources of the lights. The dark outlines of the buildings from which the glows were coming did not stand in the neat alignments of solidly unbroken rows. Here and there two or three and sometimes as many as four buildings stretched in neat lines, but on the town's two or three parallel streets gaps yawned between almost every house or store.

After a few more minutes, when Longarm reached the first of the streets and could see details clearly in spite of the fast-settling nighttime gloom, he realized that many of what he'd taken to be houses were nothing more than gutted shells. On many of them strips of paint curled down from the eaves, exposing bare wood. Doors were missing from a number of the houses; on others a door might be sagging from a single hinge or lying flat on the ground outside the house where it had fallen.

Few of the window openings in the obviously deserted houses had either glass or sashes in them. Round openings for stovepipes yawned in most of the walls, and here and there in a few of the deserted structures rusted ends of stovepipes still remained. The exterior planking of the houses that had been painted was intact on both those that were occupied and those that had been vacated, but a few of the latter had remained unpainted and wide cracks showed between the boards that formed the outer walls.

"Damned if this place ain't pretty far along to being a ghost town, old son," Longarm muttered as he glanced ahead along the deserted street. "Maybe it never was such a much to start out with, but whatever it used to be, it sure ain't got a lot left to crow about."

By this time the glow of sunset had given way to

darkness. Now Longarm could see an almost unbroken glow of light on a street that ran parallel to the one he was now following. He came to an intersecting street and reined his horse toward the glow. Nightfall was complete now, and as Longarm passed the two or three streets that intersected the one he was following and glanced along them, he could see that while more of the houses in this area were occupied, there were many gaps of blackness between them.

There was no mistaking the main street when Longarm reached it. Though there were also great gaps where storefronts had once been, and only a few pedestrians were abroad, horses stood at several of the hitch rails lining the street. Between the spaces where buildings had once stood, the lights from a half-dozen stores and the bright gleam of acetylene lamps that marked two saloons showed that life still remained in Giddings.

Ahead of him a short distance, light glinted from a public watering-trough. Longarm reined up at the oasis and dismounted. Leading his horse to the trough, he let the animal drink its fill. A few steps distant was a false-front building with swinging doors, and a horse stood at the hitch rail.

Longarm led his own mount to the rail, looped the reins of his mount beside those of the other horse there, and pushed through the batwings. He looked for the rider of the horse he'd seen outside, but except for the white-aproned barkeep lounging in a propped-back chair beside an open door at one end of the bar, the place was deserted.

Stepping up to the bar, Longarm dropped a silver dollar on the mahogany, but the coin's ringing tinkle was not needed to summon the barkeep. He'd already

111

left his chair and was moving toward Longarm.

"What's your pleasure, friend?" he asked.

Longarm's reply came automatically. "Rye. Tom Moore, if you got any."

"Can't oblige you with Moore, but how does Old Joe Gideon strike you?"

"A lot better than bourbon. And if you've got a double shotglass handy, I won't complain a bit."

"Now, that's an easy order to fill." The barkeep smiled as he reached under the bar and produced a bottle. He turned long enough to pick a shotglass from the array on the back-bar and after extracting the cork from the bottle, shoved both it and a shotglass toward Longarm.

"Name's McGinty," he said. "But my regulars call me Mac or sometimes Tex, depends on where they hail from."

"Glad to make your acquaintance, Tex. My name's Long."

"Well, since nobody else is likely to take the trouble, I'll make you welcome to Giddings," the barkeep went on. "You ride far to get here?"

"Far enough," Longarm replied. He was filling the shotglass, looking at the deep golden hue of the whiskey rising to its rim. "And I'm ready to stop a spell and catch my breath. But from what I seen of the town while I was riding through it, I don't guess there's a hotel here any longer?"

"You guessed right. And I happen to know that both of the rooming houses're full."

While McGinty was replying, Longarm lifted the shotglass and tossed off his drink. The smooth but biting rye washed most of the travel dust down his throat and left such a pleasant aftertaste that he did not hesitate in refilling the glass. He took a small sip this time before commenting on the barkeep's remark about the room shortage.

"Now, that ain't exactly what I'd call good news," he said as he lowered the glass from his lips. "I lost my hankering for sleeping on the prairie quite some time back."

"Well, you don't need to let that worry you," McGinty said. "There's plenty of vacant houses. Just pick out one where there's not anybody else dossed down and make yourself to home."

"And nobody's going to mind if I do that?"

"Who'd give two hoots in hell excepting the folks that walked away from it? And they sure ain't coming back no time soon, if they ever come back at all."

"You mind telling me what happened to the town to make folks pick up and go the way they did?"

"Why, hell's bells, it ain't no secret. Two dry years in a row and another one this year. Why, there ain't been a crop made or a herd of cattle grazed inside of near a hundred miles anyways from here."

"Well, I guess I'll just take your advice then," Longarm said. "Because it won't hurt my feelings to sleep under a roof for a change. Which way would you say I oughta head to find me an empty house?"

"Just whichever way suits you best," the barkeep replied. "It don't make that much difference. There's empty places all over Giddings just waiting for somebody to move in and make theirselves at home. If you'll look into one or two of 'em, chances are you'll find a bed and some sticks of furniture in 'em."

"And you're sure it won't matter if I—"

Longarm stopped short when the loud thwack of a

113

hand-slap sounded through the open doorway at the end of the bar and a woman came running out. She was holding one hand pressed to her cheek, and her mouth was twisted into a downward curve which could denote either anger or fear or a combination of both. She'd run halfway across the big barroom, heading for the batwings, when a man emerged from the door. He angled toward the fleeing woman, and was almost within arm's reach of her when Longarm took three distance-spanning steps and stopped between them.

"Maybe you'd best let the lady go on her way," he said. "Seems to me that's what she wants to do."

Halting in his tracks just in time to avoid colliding with Longarm, the man snarled, "You just stand outa my way, cowboy, if you know what's good for you!"

"I reckon I'm old enough to look out for myself," Longarm replied. There was no threat in the tone of his voice; his words came out as a simple factual statement.

His mouth twisting into an ugly grimace, the man flipped his right forearm, and as though through some sleight of hand the shining blade of a wicked-looking knife appeared in his hand.

"You asked for trouble!" he snapped. "Now you're going to get it!"

This was not the first time Longarm had been threatened by a knife-wielding plug-ugly. He'd worked out his own solution to the threat. Bringing up his right hand as though he was preparing to draw his Colt, he swiftly closed the fingers of his left on the hand in which the knife-wielder held his threatening blade. He pulled the other man toward him with a sudden powerful jerk, and at the same time twisted the imprisoned hand with a quick snap.

114

Caught off balance, the pain in his wrist shooting up his arm, the knife-wielder bent his knees as he tried to break free by slumping to the floor. Longarm's superior strength kept the man half-dangling as he tried to drop free, and with his right hand now closed into a fist, he landed a roundhouse swing on the other man's jaw. The blow landed solidly and his assailant went limp.

Longarm released his hold as the would-be knifer crumpled. He bent down and picked up the half-conscious man's knife. Holding it by its grip, Longarm slid the blade between his boot sole and the floor, then jerked the knife-grip sharply upward. The blade snapped and broke. Tossing the knife-grip with its inch-long blade to the floor beside its still-groggy owner, Longarm stepped back.

"You can run along now," he told the would-be carver. "And take what's left of that frog-sticker with you. It ain't good for much any more, but then you ain't either."

"I ain't going to forget this," the man snarled as he picked up the pieces of his knife. "Next time I run into you, I'll have a gun myself, and we'll see who comes out best when we're on equal terms!"

Longarm did not bother to reply to his defeated adversary's threat. He stood silently, watching the man as he swiveled on his heels and walked out of the saloon.

"I guess every town's got a few like him," he said to the barkeep. "How come you let him use your back room?"

"Because he rents it from me, just like I rent this whole shebang from the man that owns it," McGinty replied. "When times are tough the way they are now, you do what you got to if you expect to keep your place going. If I didn't rent him my back room he'd just go pay

115

somebody else for one, and I need the money as bad as the next man does."

Longarm nodded absently. He was looking around the saloon for the young woman whose appearance had started the fracas. She was nowhere to be seen; obviously she'd taken the opportunity to disappear while the dispute was going on.

"That was a nice-looking little lady," he told the saloon-keeper. "You know who she is?"

"I seen her for the first time when she come in just now," McGinty answered. "So I don't know who she is or where she come from. And I don't ask questions of anybody that rents out my back room. When times are bad, a man does what he's got to if he expects to keep going."

Again Longarm replied with a nod. While the saloon-keeper had been talking he'd walked to the bar and refilled his glass. He tossed off the drink and dropped a cartwheel on the mahogany. Hearing the coin's ring as it hit the bar, the saloon-keeper hurried to the till and made change. He dropped four dimes on the bar and shoved them across to Longarm.

"First drink was on the house," McGinty said. "You being a new customer. You figure on staying here in town?"

"Why, I can't rightly say this very minute how long I'm apt to be here," Longarm replied. "I got to do some noseying around here in the neighborhood, so I might be gone tomorrow or I might stay a few days."

"Well, stop back in whenever you take a notion. Always glad to see you."

Nodding, Longarm turned and walked to the door. Pushing through the swinging batwings, he stood in

116

front of the saloon for a moment, letting his eyes grow accustomed to the street's darkness. Scattered in the gloom a half-dozen rectangles of light spilled from the doors and windows of the small handful of stores that remained open, but along the deserted thoroughfare there were more buildings dark than the few which still showed lights inside.

Finding nothing of interest in his surroundings, Longarm freed the reins of his horse from the hitch rail and led the animal along the silent street to the nearest intersection. He looked along it, his eyes now adjusted to the gloom. The blocky outlines of houses were silhouetted against the star-filled sky in both directions. Lighted windows glowed from most of the nearby houses, but in both directions the number of houses where lights showed diminished with the distance.

Seeing that his choice would make very little difference, Longarm turned to his right and led his horse up the middle of the deserted cross-street. Moving slowly, examining each house he passed for signs that would indicate they were occupied, he had covered only a short stretch of the deserted thoroughfare before the number of houses that stood vacant exceeded those showing signs of occupancy.

By this time too, he could examine his surroundings with greater ease, for he'd reestablished his night vision during his short preliminary survey. After he'd scanned a half-dozen of the deserted houses, Longarm chose one that seemed in a bit better shape than most. Its front door was intact and its windows still had glass in all but one of the panes. He tried the knob and found that it was also locked or bolted closed from the inside.

Leading his horse to the rear of the house, he tethered

117

it to the headpiece of a brass bedstead that leaned against one wall. Then he stepped inside through the yawning rectangle that had once accommodated a door. Sliding three or four matches from his vest pocket, Longarm brought one to flame by scraping its head with his thumbnail and held it high.

Blinking in the sudden light, Longarm saw that the room he'd entered had streaked whitewashed walls and still boasted a piece of tattered Wilton carpet on the floor. One corner was filled with the rectangular form of a striped-tick mattress which oozed bits of cotton shreds from two or three slits in the ticking. A chair with one broken leg slanted in another corner. Otherwise the room was empty.

"This is about as comfortable a place as you're likely to find, old son," he said into the empty room. "You could look a long ways and do a lot worse, so you might as well settle in."

Settling in was a quick job. Longarm flicked out the match flame and stood motionless for the few moments required to let his eyes adjust to the darkness that shrouded the room after the match flickered and died. Stepping outside, he removed his horse's saddle and saddle blankets in a single load, toted the gear inside, and dropped it into a corner. He freed his own blanket roll from the saddle and spread it on the battered mattress. Pulling the broken-legged chair within easy reach of the mattress, he dropped his saddlebags onto the slanting seat and hung his hat on the back of the chair frame.

Moving a half step away from the chair, his eyes fully adjusted to the interior darkness by now, Longarm unbuckled his gunbelt and hung it across the chair's slatted back. He'd levered out of one boot and was working his leg free of the other when his horse nickered, then whinnied. Rising at once, Longarm stepped with a hobbling pace to the window and peered outside. A dark form was visible, little more than a dim shape, beside his horse.

Without wasting the time that would be needed to put on the boot he'd just taken off, Longarm slipped his Colt from its holster and hobbled to the door-opening. The dark form that he'd glimpsed from the window was still standing beside his horse. Stepping silently to the ground, Longarm took the single long step needed to bring him within arm's reach of the shapeless form. He thrust the Colt's muzzle as he moved and felt the revolver meet the shapeless figure's back.

"Just don't move," Longarm said. His voice was as cold as the Colt's steel. "This sixgun's got a hair trigger and I got a nervous trigger finger. Now, get your hands as high up as you can hold 'em and turn around so I can see who the hell you are."

Chapter 10

"Please don't shoot me!"

To Longarm's surprise the pleading voice was that of a woman. To his even greater surprise he recognized it as that of the young woman who'd fled from the man he'd confronted in the saloon. He pulled his Colt away from her head and let the weapon dangle in his lowered hand.

"I ain't about to pull the trigger on a lady," he assured her. When he spoke she turned her head in his direction, but in the darkness he could see her face only as a pale oval. He went on. "But I'm more'n a mite curious about what you're doing spying on me."

"Oh, but I'm not!" she declared. "I don't have any reason to do a thing like that!"

"Why'd you tag along after me then? You had to have some kind of idea in your head when you done it."

For a long moment Longarm's question went unanswered. At last the woman replied, "Well, I guess I followed you because I didn't have anywhere to go."

"You don't call this town home then?"

"No. I've never been here before," she went on. "And you're the only person I've run into who's been halfway kind to me since I left home to go with Grivas."

"He's the fellow in the saloon that come after me with his toad-stabber?" Longarm asked.

"Yes. He has a mean temper. I suppose you know that, though. You saw how he treated me in the saloon."

"I sure did. It wasn't what I'd call friendly—and just guessing, I'd say that's part of the reason why you got away from him?"

"Wouldn't you have done the same thing if you'd been in my position?"

"I'd likely have done more'n that," Longarm admitted. "But where'd you get off to? I looked around for you when I left the saloon, but didn't see hide nor hair of you."

"When you came outside I was hiding from him behind the corner of the building, where it was good and dark. I didn't want Grivas to see me. I was afraid he'd make me go with him someplace else."

"Why'd you come here with him in the first place?" Longarm asked, then went on quickly. "You don't need to tell me. I know how them fellows work, and whys or wherefores don't mean diddly-squat after you've done something that goes wrong."

"Well, I'd gotten over the idea of having anything else to do with him, and I was glad I stayed where I was, because he came out just a minute before you did."

"And you figured I wouldn't be no more help to you than he would've?"

122

"No. I think almost anything would've spooked me right then. So I just stayed where I was hiding, there by the saloon building, because like I said, I didn't want him to see me. He didn't even look around, though. Just got on his horse and rode off. I don't know where he went, but I sure don't want him to get hold of me again."

"Well, I can understand that," Longarm said. He was becoming aware that his bootless foot was getting chilled in the cool night breeze that had started blowing. He went on. "But there ain't any need for us to keep standing out here jawing. I ain't balanced up right to stand around, because I only got one boot on. Suppose we step inside where it'll be a mite more comfortable."

"You don't mind if I come in?"

"If I'd've minded, I wouldn't've asked you. Come along, now. There's not any more place to set down inside than there is out here, but it's warmer indoors, even in a room that ain't got no outside door to close."

They moved to the door and Longarm gave the girl a hand up to the opening, then followed her inside. The darkness was deeper in the bare little room, but the eyes of both Longarm and the girl were adjusted to the gloom by now, and the chilling breeze no longer reached them.

"I guess we can set on the floor," Longarm said. "Or on the edge of that mattress where it'd be a little softer."

Moving carefully to avoid bumping into one another in the dark room, they settled down, sitting side by side on the edge of the mattress. Longarm fished a fresh cigar out of his pocket and flicked a match into flame with his thumbnail. He was careful to close his eyes to avoid

123

being blinded as it flared brightly, but he opened them as soon as the flare vanished. While he held the flame to the tip of his long thin cheroot, he eyed the young woman who'd settled down beside him.

He got only a fleeting glimpse of her in the moment or two required to puff his cigar alight, but accustomed as he was to registering quick impressions of people and places, he saw that she was a bit older than he'd taken her to be when he first saw her in the saloon. At that time, he'd been paying more attention to the man called Grivas than he had to her.

With the illumination of the flickering match flame Longarm saw that she had regular features: high cheekbones in an elongated oval face, an aquiline nose slightly tilted at the tip, full red lips, and a firm chin. He also noted that her breasts swelled firmly rounded in a low-cut dress.

He was raising his arm to lift the burning match and get a better light from it when the flame reached his fingertips and he was forced to extinguish it quickly. For a moment the room was plunged into an almost stygian darkness; then as he puffed his cigar, the glowing coal at its tip made the room seem brighter than before.

"How'd you happen to find me here?" he asked. "Or follow me—because I reckon that's what you done."

"Well, when you left the saloon, I was standing there behind the corner of the building. Grivas had just ridden off and—I guess I followed you because I didn't have anywhere to go. And because you'd helped me, I suppose."

"You ought've called me instead of just tagging along

after me," Longarm said. "But I got to admit you done a pretty good job of trailing me, because I sure didn't catch on that you was following me."

"I—I wasn't really thinking about anything more than getting away from Grivas," she admitted hesitantly. "If I'd've had a gun, I think I'd've shot that no-good liar who was trying to make me whore for him."

"You ain't in that kinda life regular then?"

She shook her head. Then speaking even more slowly than before she went on. "I don't guess I need to tell you that I'm not—well, not innocent like I used to be a long time ago. But I never have been—oh, you know what I'm trying to say."

"I reckon I do," Longarm said. "You got a name, I suppose?"

"It's Lillian," she replied. "At least, that's what my folks named me. But everybody generally calls me Lily."

"Well, Lily, my name's Long. I'm a deputy United States marshal, and I come here on a case."

"Then—why're you spending the night in a place like this?" Lily's voice conveyed the frown that by the faint light from his cigar Longarm could see forming on her face. "If you're a United States marshal like you say you are, I'm sure you've got the money to pay for a room."

"Oh, I ain't short for money, and I could sure use my badge to get a room, even if things are crowded as that barkeep said they was. But I ain't about to turn somebody out of a room they've paid for just because I got a badge and they haven't."

"So you came and found this place instead," she said. "But there must be another reason."

"On account of if I went flashing my badge at a rooming house it'd be all over town in ten minutes that I'm here looking to arrest somebody. Once the news spread around, the man I'm after'd just hightail it away before I had a chance to catch up with him."

"I hadn't thought about that," Lily said. "But I can see that you're right about what would happen."

"And I reckon you didn't have the money to go rent a room with, so you just figured to tag along after me?" Longarm asked.

"Oh, I'm not really hard up for money. I've still got a few dollars that I brought with me from home."

"But you didn't go looking for a room either," Longarm pointed out.

"No, because I'd heard what the saloon-keeper told Grivas about there being no rooms in town. I couldn't think of anywhere to go after I left the saloon, so when you came out I followed you. I had an idea you'd find a place to sleep, and I figured that you'd be a lot better to me than he ever was."

"Well, now, Lily, it looks like we're both up the same creek without a canoe or a paddle," Longarm said. "And I'd guess you must be about as tired as I am. Why don't we just go to sleep now? In the morning I'll see about finding some way to get you home, then I'll get busy on my own job. I need to work on the case I'm here on and see can I get it closed up."

"Anything you say," she told him. "But don't worry about me. I'm old enough to take care of myself, so I promise you that I won't be any trouble to you or get in the way of whatever your job might be."

"Let's wait to talk about that in the morning," Longarm suggested. As he spoke he was removing his gunbelt. He folded it carefully to put the holster on top, and laid the belt down in a position beside the mattress that would allow him to draw the Colt instantly. Putting his hat under his head for a pillow, he stretched out and relaxed. Lily, lying beside him, had followed his movements as best she could in the darkness. She too stretched out now, and they fell silent, lying motionless, inches apart.

Longarm's day had been a busy one, and soon he was sleeping soundly. He had no idea how long he'd slept when Lily stirred on the mattress beside him and he woke instantly. He did not stir or speak, but through slitted eyes he could see her dimly as she leaned over him. The white oval of her face and the blurred outline of her full lips registered on his night-hampered vision before she moved and he could no longer see her. Then he felt the gentle touch of her hand at his groin.

Longarm did not stir. He continued to feign sleep while Lily's fingers moved gently across his hips, then softly slid lower. He felt her fingers, as light as the touch of a butterfly's wings, as she slid them even lower and began to stroke his crotch.

Now that he had a hint of what to expect, Longarm relaxed and continued to lie motionless while she busied her fingers solving the problem of unbuttoning his trousers' fly. She discovered the way to slip the buttons free easily. Then Longarm felt the warmth of her skin as her hand slid into the folds of his balbriggans to liberate him completely.

Lily held his flaccid cylinder cupped in one of her warm hands for a moment while with her free hand she began to stroke him with soft careful strokes of her fingertips. Then she bent down, and after a moment or two of the caresses she now administered with the tip of her agile tongue, Longarm no longer held back, but released the firm control he'd been exercising. He gave way to his body's urging and allowed himself to become completely erect. Lily bent lower now to bring her lips and moist warm tongue into full play. After what seemed a long time had passed, she finally engulfed him completely.

Longarm did not move or speak for several minutes. Then he said softly, "I reckon you know how good that makes a man feel, but it's about time you begun to pleasure yourself."

"I was just waiting for you wake up enough to invite me," Lily replied. "And if you hadn't, I'd've invited myself."

As she spoke, Lily was shrugging out of her dress. Her camisole followed her dress, cascading to the floor. While Longarm watched the completion of her undressing, he rid himself of his shirt and unbuttoned his longjohns, removing them at the same time that he was stepping out of his trousers.

Longarm lay back on the bed. His erection was jutting and full now and he waited for Lily to join him, but she did not lie down beside him. Instead, she rose to straddle Longarm's hips. She held herself above him only long enough to place him before lowering herself on his rock-firm shaft until his full penetration was completed. She squirmed for a moment or two, sighing happily, then began rocking her hips.

Longarm clasped her waist with his big muscular hands and caught her rhythm; then each time she reached the apex of her upward levering, he pulled her to him with a quick downward jerk accompanied by an upthrust of his hips. Lily's soft moans soon became babbles of delight, and these quickly turned into bursts of pleased high-pitched sighs that escaped her lips as his upthrust stroke ended with the fleshly thwack of their bodies colliding.

Under the pressure of his fingers Longarm could feel the beginning ripples of Lily's body which told him that her completion was beginning. Stopping his rhythmic stroking, he released his grip on her hips and wrapped his arms around her. Pulling her to him and holding her close, her full breasts crushed against his muscular chest, he turned them together on the mattress without breaking their fleshly bond.

For several moments Longarm did not move, but lay quietly with his body poised above her as he waited for the beginning pulsations that were rippling through Lily's body to subside. When her small preliminary tremors had faded and she lay quietly, her body still tense, Longarm began stroking again, slowly and deliberately. Lily locked her legs around his hips and dug her heels into Longarm's buttocks each time he drove in with his rhythmic downward thrusts.

For a long while time seemed suspended in the darkened room, its quietness broken only by the faint impacts of flesh on flesh, then a small moan began bubbling in Lily's throat. Longarm took his cue from the almost inaudible bubbles of sound. He drove with more vigor and instead of setting a faster pace, he held back the beginning of his penetrations for a few seconds longer while Lily's moans grew deeper in tone and her body began to quiver involuntarily.

When her quivers grew spastic and her moans burst from her throat oftener and grew louder, Longarm stepped up the tempo of his driving. He no longer waited for a moment after completing a thrust before starting another deep full drive. Lily's body began twitching as her climax grew closer. Longarm did not allow himself to share her frenzy this time, but drove on until her throaty cries rose without interruption and her body's twitching became an uninterrupted spasm.

Suddenly she screamed and shook violently and her back arched as her legs tightened around Longarm's hips. Her scream faded to a hoarse whisper, and Longarm drove with a final thrust and held himself pressed closely to her while she writhed and shuddered and the shudders peaked and died away. When her body suddenly went limp Longarm held himself pressed close against her, his lips pressing hers, until her pulsations faded and died away and she lay spent.

Neither of them moved for several minutes, their breathing the only sound that broke the night's quiet in the little room. Lily stirred first, a soft experimental motion of her hips. Then she looked up at him and said in a voice just above a whisper, "I never have had a romp in bed with a man like you before, but I guess your kind's few and far between. I feel like a frazzle, but I can still feel you in me, and I've got the idea you're ready to start again."

"I am if you figure you're feeling up to it."

"To tell you the truth, I don't know how I feel, but if you're ready to start I'll stay with you to the finish."

Instead of replying, Longarm began his slow deep stroking once again. Lily was slower in responding, but as he continued driving, her arousal grew, and soon she was joining him as lustily as before. Minutes ticked off into infinity, and when at last time caught up with them and the aftermath of their frenzies passed, they sighed and slept, still in a close embrace.

"I guess we'd better say good-bye now, Longarm," Lily said.

They were sitting on the mattress in the gray morning light that preceded sunrise, finishing the breakfast they'd shared from the scant supply of trail food that Longarm carried in his saddlebags.

"You going someplace?" Longarm asked.

"Back home," she replied. "Just from the little bit I saw of Giddings last night I could tell that it's a dying town."

"You called the turn on that card," Longarm agreed. "I've see towns die too. But what're you aiming to do when you get home?"

"I don't know yet," Lily admitted as she stood up. "But from what I saw yesterday, I don't suppose I'd be able to find a job in a town like this that's running down, unless it's the kind of job Grivas had in mind for me, and I don't want that. I guess I'll just do what I've been doing, help all I can around the place and hope something good will happen."

"Well, I wish I had an answer for you, but I can't come up with one offhand," Longarm said. "Except I hate to just walk away—"

"Don't," she broke in. "It's up to me to do the walking away because I'm the one who followed you here. You just sit still and finish breakfast. By the time you're back on your own job, I'll be well on my way."

His gear stowed away again in his saddlebags, Longarm swung into the saddle and turned his mount in the direction of the only street in Giddings with which he was familiar. In daylight he could see the town's deterioration more clearly than he'd been able to the night before.

A few quick glances as he rode along the deserted street were all that he needed to confirm the silent story he'd sensed the night before. It was plain that at one time the street had been solidly lined with stores and offices, but gaps now yawned where some of the structures had been removed or razed, and a number of those that still stood were shuttered, their show windows bare and their doors padlocked.

When he reached the saloon where he'd run into Lily the night before, Longarm reined up at the hitch rail, tethered his horse, and pushed through the swinging doors. At one end of the long bar McGinty was asleep in a chair that he'd tilted back for comfort.

Stepping up to the bar, Longarm tossed a silver dollar on its surface. The ringing tinkle of the coin brought the barkeep wide awake. The front legs of his chair hit the floor with a thunk and he stood up, rubbing his eyes as he turned toward Longarm.

"Well, friend, glad to see you back," McGinty said. As he stepped behind the long stretch of mahogany he went on. "Guess you'll be wanting an eye-opener. Same as last night, I take it?"

"You take it right," Longarm replied. "And maybe you can help me find a man I'm looking for."

"I might if you know what his name is," McGinty said as he reached for the bottle of rye whiskey on the back-bar. He went over to Longarm, fumbled beneath the bar a moment, and produced a shotglass. As he filled it after placing it in front of Longarm he went on. "Except

132

there's been a lot of folks leave town of late, and this fellow you're looking for might be one of 'em."

"Might be at that," Longarm agreed. Before going on he put a half-dollar on the bar and took a swallow of the pungent whiskey. As he set down the half-emptied glass he continued. "But if you been here a while, you'd know whether he's still around. His name's Longley."

Chapter 11

For a moment McGinty stared openmouthed at Longarm, then he smiled and asked, "You're out to josh me,
ain't you, friend?"

"Not so's you'd notice," Longarm answered. "I don't
see nothing funny about just calling a man's name. It's
Longley I'm looking for, just like I said it."

His smile fading, the saloon man went on. "No, I can
see you're not the kind to be took in, like some. But
that being the case, you oughta know that old Wild Bill
Longley's been dead and buried long enough for every
bounty-hunter in the country to know about it. Besides,
you talk too smart and you don't look ornery and hungry
enough to be a bounty-hunter."

"No, that sure ain't my line," Longarm agreed. "And
when I say Longley, I don't mean Wild Bill. Now, I
don't want a lot of talk getting started, so I'm going to
ask you to just sorta forget what I'm about to say."

"From the way I got you cased, you've been around long enough to know that nobody in the saloon business is going to talk about anything a customer tells him private."

"That's what I'm counting on," Longarm said. "So I'll make it short and sweet. My name's Long, Custis Long. I'm a deputy United States marshal outa the Denver office, but I'm doing a special job here in Texas for Judge Parker, over in Little Rock. I expect you've heard about him?"

"I don't guess there's many folks in this part of the world that hasn't heard about him," McGinty answered.

"And seeing you live in Giddings, I'd say you know as much about the Longleys as the next man."

"I know what the townfolks have been saying," the saloon-keeper said. "Except that now since Wild Bill Longley's dead and gone, nobody talks a lot about 'em any more."

"The family don't make much of a stir then?"

"Not so's you'd notice. Oh, now and again there'll be some chatter pass around—that seems to go with the family name. But when there's talk passing back and forth anymore, it's generally always about Wild Bill and his outlaw ways and how he walked away from being strung up down south of here—in Karnes City, I guess it was—along with one of his horse-thief friends."

"You don't need to dot no *i*'s nor cross no *t*'s," Longarm broke in. "I know about him too, even if I never happened to butt heads with him."

"Then you'd know he sort of settled down after he'd killed that preacher up in Delta County. I guess he figured coming all the way down here to the middle

136

part of Texas he'd put enough miles behind him so the law'd miss finding him."

Longarm nodded. "That's where he was wrong. He wasn't no different than most outlaws in not giving the law enough credit. But he put in quite a spell free and clear after he slipped away from up north. I guess he was here most of that time?"

"Why, the first thing he did was bring his folks here. There was his daddy and mama, they're both dead now. And somewheres along the way Wild Bill had got married, and him and his wife had a boy, that's Harland. Of course, by now Harland's boy's about grown up, and Harland named him after his grandpa."

"And the family stayed here after Wild Bill had got caught up with and hanged?" Longarm asked.

"They sure did," McGinty replied. "From what I heard a good long spell ago, they didn't have much else of a place to go. You see, Wild Bill had sorta settled down here in Giddings till the law finally caught up with him. They gave him another trial right here in Giddings, and he got found guilty and they strung him up again. Now, I know there's a lot of folks believe he walked away from the second necktie party just like he did from the first one, but it just ain't a fact."

"From the way you talk, you know as much about him as I do, maybe more," Longarm observed.

Ignoring the comment as though Longarm had not spoken, the barkeep went on. "Anyways, what's left of old Wild Bill Longley's kin ain't outlaws, like the old boy hisself was."

"It ain't the old Wild Bill that I got on my mind right this minute. What-all can you tell me about the place the Longley family's got hereabouts?"

"There's not a lot to tell," McGinty answered. "The little spread they've got is out to the east of town. It'd be the third one you'd get to, if you're going out there. All the Longleys I know about but one lives there."

"What about the one that don't live there?" Longarm asked.

"That'd be Harland, he's old Bill's boy. After he'd got pretty much grown up he didn't live here for a spell, then he moved back. But the funny thing about it is, he didn't stay at the family place, even if his wife and boy still lives out there. First thing anybody knew he was living here in town again, and he still does."

"You got any idea about why he moved away from his folks?" Longarm asked. "The family have trouble? Some kind of split-up that wound up with him moving?"

"Not that me or anybody else I know has heard about. He could've moved just lately, but there's nary a one of the Longleys that'll talk about the other ones, and none of 'em talks about their business."

"Closemouthed, are they?"

"Every last one of 'em," McGinty agreed.

"So what you've told me is all you know about 'em?"

"It's about as much as anybody knows, when push comes to shove. I'd guess old Bill's boy left on account of some kind of family fuss, but the only ones that'd know all the whys and wherefores would be one of the Longley's theirselves."

"Well, go ahead and tell me about the one Longley that lives here in town," Longarm suggested.

"Harland? Well, since he's the only boy anybody knows about Wild Bill having, there's some folks here in town that call him Young Bill, but he don't like that,

138

says it's not his name, that's what he named his boy," the barkeep said.

"And you said Harland just up and moved into town," Longarm noted. Then he asked, "Still lives here, I guess?"

"Oh, sure. I reckon it was about the time when he moved into town away from the family place—and that's been quite a spell back—the town councilmen hired him on here to be chief of police. The town was a lot different then, but the way Harland did his job didn't set too well with some of the townfolks."

"Meaning his feet got too big and he begun stepping on folks' toes?" Longarm frowned.

"Oh, he did more'n that," McGinty replied. He was silent for a moment, as though trying to find the words he needed to explain. At last he shrugged and said, "Maybe the best way I can put it is that some folks thought he was a little bit sixgun happy. Anyway, the councilmen upped and taken the job away from him."

"And he didn't go back to live with his kinfolks?"

"Not him. He put in a little butcher shop in town here; it's just a ways up the street."

"How'd he figure to make a go of it, if nobody in town liked him? Seems like to me they wouldn't've bought much."

For a moment McGinty studied the middle distance, then he said slowly, "Now, that's a funny thing. You'd've thought that if nobody liked him when he was being a policeman, they wouldn't buy off of him. But they did. From what I've seen and heard, he's got a pretty good trade going for him by now."

Accustomed as he'd become to surprises during the years he'd been a lawman, Longarm could barely conceal

139

his astonishment while he was listening to the unexpected information. To give himself a moment in which to think, he swallowed about half the contents of the shotglass McGinty had filled while they were talking.

"And he runs the butcher shop without any of his kinfolks helping him?" Longarm asked after he'd put away the swallow.

"Well, his boy does help him a little bit. Keeps the shop neatened up, drives the little delivery cart, looks after trade when Harland's gone—like he was a little while back, all the things like that."

"I didn't hear you say whether or not he's got a wife."

"Well, he used to have. It's been a coon's age since I seen her. Last I heard she was living out at the family place, and so was Young Bill. And I never heard anybody come right out flat-footed and say she'd left him."

"A minute ago, you said the rest of the Longleys was all dead?" Longarm frowned. "I guess you're sure about that?"

"That's right. I guess Harland was the only younker Wild Bill ever had. Leastways, I never heard about him having any more."

"If anybody has heard, I'd imagine it'd be hometown folks like you and the other ones that lives here," Longarm suggested.

"I imagine," the barkeep agreed.

"Which means you'd be pretty sure to know."

"Not just me, but everybody else, hometown folks, like you said a minute ago. Giddings ain't all that big of a place no more. Everybody knows everybody else. It's sorta like the town's just one big family."

Longarm nodded. He picked up his half-emptied glass and drained it. When he set it back on the bar and made no move to refill it, McGinty gestured toward the bottle.

"You ain't having but one?" he asked. "I guess you know what they say, a man can't walk good on just one leg."

"I've heard it a time or two," Longarm replied. "But I got my horse outside, so one good leg's all I need. I'll likely be back to get another sip after a while to balance me off."

Swinging into the saddle of his mount, Longarm rode down Giddings's still-deserted main street. Once again, he could see the full extent of the little town's desolation.

Where stores had once stood to form an unbroken line along the main street, gaps now showed where buildings had been torn down or moved to a new location or another town. There were untidy higgledy-piggledy heaps of split and splintered weathered planks that marked the places where a few of the older abandoned structures had been allowed to decay until they collapsed.

Some of them, spaced between the ruins and the indications of a building's removal, simply had their windows and doors boarded over. A number of the buildings which were still in use needed paint, and on some of them split or warped boards signaled the need of replacement. The signs above many of the surviving stores needed repainting, but on several of them the names of the stores or their proprietors had been painted over and new names painted on the blocked-out areas. However, a number of these were also shuttered and closed.

A few of the buildings had received the sort of treatment others lacked. Their shining fronts glowed with fresh paint and most of them bore newly lettered signs. They glowed like beacons amid the majority on which deterioration, desertion, or neglect had laid a heavy hand. It was one of these few which bore the sign: "H. LONGLEY BUTCHER SHOP."

There was no hitch rail in front of the shop. Longarm draped the reins of his mount over the hitch rail of the shuttered, deserted building next door and stepped back to the butcher shop. Through the spotlessly clean window he saw a young man, busy at a butcher block behind the short counter, wrapping cuts of meat. Moving on to the door, he went inside.

Before Longarm could speak the youth looked up from his work at the butcher block and said, "If you're a customer come looking to buy fresh meat, mister, I'm sorry, but I got to tell you right off that every bit of it on the place is already spoke for. All there'll be till day after tomorrow is ham or bacon or salt-back. And I've got a stick of summer sausage that's ripe enough to be cut."

"I ain't figuring to buy anything right now," Longarm told him. "My name's Long. Deputy U.S. marshal. I'm looking for this Longley fellow who's got his name on that sign outside."

"That's my father's name. My name is William."

Longarm choked back the question that formed in his mind, but made a mental note to ask the key question later. He acknowledged the youth's reply with a nod as he glanced around the interior of the little butcher shop. He saw no closets, no other doors except the back door which stood ajar, giving him a glimpse of the alley behind the store.

"And he ain't here right now," Longarm said. "I can see that for myself. But I'd imagine you know where I can find him."

"Of course," the young man answered. "He's gone to

142

the family place. It's a little ways outside of town."

"You reckon he'll be back pretty soon then?"

"It's not very likely, Marshal Long. This is slaughter day. He's got a steer to kill. Then he'll have to hang it to bleed a while before he can gut it and skin it out. After that he'll have to quarter it. He'll bring the carcass in here to cut the meat orders, and then I'll wrap them and deliver them. I don't look for him to get back today, but you'll likely find him here tomorrow morning. He usually comes in early and I come in later. But maybe I can help you. My name's William Longley."

Longarm did not reply directly to the young man. "I guess your mother's most likely out there at your family place too?"

"Of course."

"Then I guess I better go out and see can I find him," Longarm said thoughtfully.

"Is there something wrong, or something I can help you with, Marshal Long?"

"I don't reckon there is," Longarm answered. "Except that I'd be obliged if you'll tell me how I can get to this family place you mentioned."

"Just follow the main street east. It turns into the road at the end of town. Go on past the first two spreads—you can see the main houses of both of them from the road—and ours is the third one you'll come to."

"Well, I ought not to have any trouble," Longarm said. "Now, if you'll just cut me off a pretty-good-sized chunk of that summer sausage, I'll be on my way."

Back in the saddle, Longarm toed his mount into motion and reined the animal onto the street.

• • •

Longarm let his horse set its own gait as he rode through the steadily warming midday air. The day was well along by now, and he no longer had to slant his head downward to keep the sun out of his eyes. He shifted his gaze from one section of the green but deserted landscape to another as his jaws worked steadily, chewing hungrily on the big hunk of summer sausage he'd just bitten off.

A short time ago Longarm had passed one of the two spreads he'd been told to look for, a house and a small cluster of barns and sheds set well back from the road. Now he squinted ahead, looking for the second. Before he saw it on the crest of one of the low green hills that formed the ragged horizon-line, he'd eaten two more bites of the sausage and was working on another.

"Folks here can say what they want to, old son," he told himself silently as his jaws worked on the spicy meat. "But Texas is just too damned big of a place. You start out to go somewheres and you feel like you oughta be meeting yourself coming back before you've got halfway to where you was heading for when you begun."

Longarm was nearly abreast of the second spread now. Like the first ranch he'd passed, this one was also a cluster of utility buildings, barns and sheds and stables, seemingly placed at random around a low-roofed main house. Squinting at the sun, now passing its zenith, he wiped his lips on the back of his hand and fumbled a cigar out of his vest pocket. Trailing a thin plume of smoke that dissipated quickly in the clear air, he set his eyes ahead again, looking for the third spread, the clump of buildings that would mark the end of his ride.

They appeared a bit sooner than he'd expected. Nestling near the crest of a low rise and still three or four miles distant, a house dwarfed by a huge rambling barn took shape. It was on another upslope which rose above the low down-slanted section of the road which Longarm was now covering. He kept his gaze fixed on the buildings now, looking for some sign of activity in their vicinity. From the angle at which he was approaching all that he could make out was that the barn's door was open and a tethered horse stood just outside it.

While he was completing his examination of the big barn and the horse standing motionless in front of it, a flicker of motion from the house drew Longarm's attention. He gave his full attention to the house now, and had been examining it for only a moment when two people, a man and a woman, came out and started toward the barn. The distance between Longarm and the pair was still so great that the couple looked like puppets on a miniature stage, responding to the strings pulled by someone who was hidden from view.

Before they'd gotten halfway to the huge barn the couple stopped. Even at the distance which still remained between him and the buildings, Longarm could see that the two who'd emerged from the house were engaged in some sort of argument. He'd gotten quite a bit closer, but as he dipped into another drop in the road he lost sight of the pair.

When he began mounting the rise beyond the dip, the couple had gotten almost to the huge barn. Just before reaching it they stopped. The woman grabbed the man's arm, and though he lifted it slightly in his effort to pull away from her, she held fast. If their argument had ever stopped, it continued now, and indeed seemed to take on a freshly inspired life.

They'd stopped on the winding downsloping path,

facing each other. The man had given up his attempt to pull his arm free, perhaps because the woman had now clasped both hands around the man's forearm. He was gesticulating with his free hand, and though neither of them was facing the direction from which Longarm was approaching, at some point in their heated discussion the woman turned away from the man, and in her movement caught sight of Longarm.

Turning back to her companion, she pointed toward the road. Following his usual custom when on a long ride, Longarm had returned to letting his mount set its own pace. Now he prodded the animal's flanks again with his boot toe, and obediently the horse began picking up its gait. Just ahead of him the road dipped into one of its many low stretches, and for a few moments Longarm lost sight of the pair in front of the house as he rode downslope through the broad valley and started up the next rise.

Topping the upslope in the road at last, Longarm could see at once that the man and woman standing between the buildings he was fast approaching were continuing their heated argument. She'd lost her two-handed grip, but still held the man's arm with one hand while gesticulating with the other. By now Longarm was close enough to see that the jaws of both of them were wagging vigorously and that the man was grossly fat, his body almost twice the size of the woman's slender frame. The man was still attempting to pull his arm from her grasp, but she was clinging to it doggedly.

Returning his attention to the road, Longarm noted that only one more dip leading to a final hump remained in it between him and the arguing pair. He glanced around, his eyes flicking across the terrain ahead, looking for a place where he could leave the road and cut cross-country to get to his destination more quickly.

At the point he'd reached now, the brush along the roadside was unusually thick. He could see no easy and sure way to break through it in less time than he'd spend by staying on the road. He prodded his tiring horse a bit harder than usual, and the animal picked up its pace as it headed down into the shallow dip.

Chapter 12

For a moment Longarm again lost sight of the arguing couple as the road made an unexpected jog to avoid the precipitously yawning cleft of a deep narrow arroyo that forced the wide trail into a sharp bend. He'd been keeping track of his progress, and waited impatiently for his horse to finish the jog and turn back. He then began to mount the road's final long upslope, and when at last he topped the rise and the pair ahead came into sight again, Longarm saw that they had separated.

Now the woman was standing alone on the narrow trail that ran from the house to the barn, while the fat man was running in a weaving waddle in the direction of the barn. In spite of his bulk, he was moving fast. Even across the distance that still separated him from the silent panorama, Longarm could see clearly that the man was going to attain his objective—either the shelter of the barn or the saddled horse—for only now did the woman overcome her surprise or indecision and start after him.

Once more Longarm looked for a place to break through the brushy barrier along the edges of the narrow road. He could find no spot where penetrating the high green growth would be a quick and easy job. He returned his attention to the couple standing between the house and barn, though neither was standing still now. The man had almost reached the barn; then the woman put on a desperate spurt and almost caught up with him before the fat man reached the horse and pulled its reins free.

Longarm drummed his boot heels on the sides of his mount, but the horse was fading again. It responded with only a slight burst of speed, then it slowed on the final upslope. Though it made a valiant effort, the animal responded so slowly and reluctantly that Longarm saw at once it would be impossible for him to reach the barn in time to stop the fat man from leaving. The buildings were still some distance ahead, near the top of another gentle rise in the ground.

Longarm looked at the woman. The effort she was making had put her almost within reach of the man. He was yanking the horse's reins around to put it in position for him to mount, and a single quick glance told Longarm that there was no possible way he could reach the fat man in time to stop him from getting into the saddle. Even though it was now plain that the distance to the ranch buildings was too great for him to span before the fat man could ride off, Longarm did not give up his last-ditch effort.

Forced to watch helplessly while the man swung into the saddle, Longarm saw the fleeing rider dig his heels into the horse's flanks and, after covering the short distance to the road, rein the horse into it and kick it into a gallop. At the barn, the woman stood gazing after the fleeing man.

Longarm realized at once that the man's move brought him face-to-face with a new decision. He could spur his tiring horse ahead and chase after the fleeing rider, or he could stop and try to get some information from the woman regarding the fat man's destination. The woman was looking from Longarm to the departing rider, who by this time was vanishing in one of the road's many dips.

Taking the first of his two choices, Longarm studied the direction the fleeing man was taking and set out in pursuit. In his long experience as a lawman he'd learned that only those who have something to fear are quick to panic and run. However, he was also aware that a tiring horse had little chance of overtaking a fresh one.

Bit by bit the distance between Longarm and the galloping rider ahead grew greater as the chase continued. The fugitive was still following the road. Now he looked back as though to judge how much of a lead he'd managed to get. Though Longarm had neither gained nor lost ground, he was not surprised when he saw the man ahead rein his horse off the road and set out on a long slanting course across the hillocky humps of the prairie, his direction still continuing to take him further from the ranch house.

Longarm's horse was beginning to tire now. He seldom loosed warning shots at a fugitive, and now hesitated to shoot at the fleeing man, for he knew of no reason for his flight. But he drew his Colt reluctantly and let off a warning shot into the air. The fugitive still did not stop.

Even after Longarm had loosed two more shots in his effort to bring the man to a halt, the rider ahead maintained his steady pace. Longarm was dissatisfied with his inability to catch up with his quarry, but realized that he had little chance of overtaking the man ahead in a chase across open country familiar to the fugitive.

Despite the fact that the man was at the very edge of effective pistol range, Longarm brought up his Colt again and emptied it this time. He aimed low, seeking to wound the horse, but he saw his slugs raise dust puffs from the ground behind the galloping animal. Disgusted with his poor shooting, Longarm reined in.

His tired horse was panting now and trembling from the exhaustion of the prolonged chase. Longarm watched his escaping quarry, marking the fleeing man's direction in his mind, then reined his horse around and followed the undulating road to the beaten track leading to the big barn. He pulled up a short distance from the waiting woman and without dismounting, touched his hat brim in greeting.

"I seen you and that fellow riding away was having some kind of disagreement, ma'am," he said. "You seen me take after him and—"

"I heard you shooting at him too," the woman broke in angrily.

"Well, he was plumb outa range when I done the shooting," Longarm told her. "And I knew I didn't have a Chinaman's chance of hitting him. I was just trying to get him to stop. Now, if that little fracas you and him was having was over something private between the two of you that I ain't got no business butting into, I don't aim to pay it no mind. But I'm a law officer, and if he's robbed you or hurt you, I'll take after him again and run him down and see that he goes to the lockup."

"You don't have anything to worry about. It was just a little disagreement between the two of us," she replied, then added quickly, "I'd imagine you know how it is when a husband and wife get into a quarrel."

"Well, I don't know from being a husband myself," Longarm said. "Seeing as how I ain't got a wife to fuss with. But I've seen enough family spats to know that it ain't real smart for somebody outside of the family to go and butt into 'em. I'm sorry I was so nosey, but I guess—"

"You did just what any other man would've done, I'm sure," she said. If she'd been disturbed by the obvious quarrel she and the man had been having, or if she was still angry because of Longarm's earlier actions, it did not show in her voice as she went on. "But I'm certain that I've never seen you around here before."

"No, ma'am. I just got into town yesterday. You see, I'm a lawman, and—"

"You don't tell me!" she interrupted. "Well! It's certainly time we got somebody here in Lee County to keep law and order! Why, for the last six months we haven't had a sheriff or even a deputy, and the county judge dying sort of unexpected last month didn't make things any better. It'll be an improvement to have you, even if you're new on the job."

"Well, I wouldn't say I was exactly new on my job," Longarm replied. "Because you sorta got what I said mixed up. I ain't a deputy sheriff for the county here. I'm a deputy United States marshal working outa the Denver office."

"I guess I didn't understand," she said. "But it doesn't

matter all that much, and I'll still stand by what I just said about this county."

"They'll likely get around to hiring somebody to keep things in hand," Longarm said. "I've seen it happen before, even if this is sorta new country to me. It's the first time my work's ever brought me to Giddings or anyplace close by in this part of Texas. And I guess I ought've started out by telling you my name. It's Custis Long."

"So you were just riding by and stopped to see if you could be of any help to me," she went on without bothering to acknowledge his introduction or to identify herself in turn. "That was very thoughtful of you, Marshal Long, and I appreciate your offer of help, even though I don't need any."

"Then maybe you'll give me a little bit of help," Longarm went on. "I'm looking for the Longley place."

"Well, you've found it. I'm Mabel Longley. That man you saw riding away was my husband, Harland. But I can't imagine what sort of business you'd have with either of us."

While they talked, Longarm had been taking stock of the woman. She was almost as tall as he was, slim and angular. Her face was thin, her deep-set eyes a dark brown under sparse brows. Her nose was aquiline, the tip cut sharply back below her slightly flared nostrils. Her chin was rounded and firm, but at first glance it gave an impression of weakness.

She had a habit, whenever she stopped speaking, of compressing her thin lips into a narrow, straight, and almost invisible line. Her high prominent cheekbones were covered by tight-stretched skin that was tanned to a deep brown. Her hands showed that they were

154

accustomed to hard work. The skin on their backs was a deeper brown than her face, and lined like a sheet of wet brown paper that had been crinkled into a ball, then spread out flat to dry.

"Why, there's a thing or two I need to talk over with your husband," Longarm replied. "I wasn't just riding by your place when I pulled in. I was aiming to stop here anyways, even if it did look to me like you and that man who just rode off was having a bit of a fuss."

"Married couples argue quite often, Marshal," she replied a bit tartly. "That little spat we were having upset him, and I'm sure that my husband's reason for riding away wasn't just to end our argument, but to avoid being embarrassed by having to explain it to a stranger."

"Well, now," Longarm said. "That just means I'm going to have to ask you to tell me where he might've taken off for, because I need to talk to him soon as I can catch up with him."

"What sort of business could you possibly have with him?" she asked. "I'm sure he hasn't been anywhere near Denver. As a matter of fact, he's been here for—well, quite a long while, except for a short trip that he took a few weeks ago."

"What I ain't got around to explaining yet is that right now I'm on detached duty outa my regular station," Longarm went on. "I'm doing a little bit of work for Judge Parker, up at Fort Smith, in Arkansas."

"That's as far away as Denver," she quickly pointed out. "And I'm sure that Harland hasn't been there either."

"Now, ma'am, I ain't accusing your husband of doing anything that's against the law. I won't do that till I dig

155

a lot deeper into my case," Longarm went on. "But it don't have a thing to do with Denver or Fort Smith, and anyways I ought not to stand here and be bothering you about it. Maybe you can tell me where your husband might be heading?"

"Why—into town, I'd imagine," she replied. "I'm sure you know that's where his meat market is."

"Yes, ma'am. Matter of fact, that's where I started out to your place from. Your boy William told me I'd likely find his daddy here."

"William isn't my son, Marshal Long. He's my step-son, even though I do try to treat him like he was my own flesh and blood. But are you suggesting that Harland and William are working together in some sort of—well, that they're doing something that's against the law?"

Longarm replied quickly, "Now, ma'am, I ain't suggesting anything at all. And I won't until—"

Before he could finish what he'd started to say, Mabel Longley interrupted. "Except for the little butcher shop my husband's got in town, we're just plain ranchers. And if you're thinking that because—"

"Now, hold on for a minute, if you don't mind, ma'am," Longarm interrupted in turn. His voice was sharper this time as he went on. "I told you that I don't know of a thing right now that'd I'd arrest anybody for. All I want to do is to ask them some questions about this case I'm working on."

"Suppose you tell me what sort of case it is you're talking about," she suggested. "Just on the outside chance it might be something I could help you with."

Longarm did not answer her for a moment, then he shook his head as he said, "My case ain't tied into anything that might've happened here in Giddings, Miz

Longley. I guess the best thing for me to do is head back to town and see if I can find your husband or your boy. They're the ones I need to talk to."

"Please don't think I'm just being inquisitive, as women are supposed to be. And I'm not trying to interfere with your case, Marshal Long, whatever or whoever it might involve," she told him, her voice firm. "But unless you object very strongly, I'm going to ride into Giddings with you. And I hope you won't mind if I insist on being present during any conversation you might have with either my husband or my son."

"I sure won't, ma'am," Longarm assured her. "But what you need to understand is that I ain't been sent here to judge anybody. The case I'm on is murder, and until I find out a lot more'n I know right now, all I'm figuring on doing is ask questions."

"Murder!" she exclaimed. "Why, neither Harland or William would raise a hand to anybody!" She paused for a moment. "You're sure you didn't get the idea to come out looking for them just because of the reputation Harland's father had? And since you're a lawman, you'd likely know who I'm talking about."

"Well, I ain't one to beat around the bush," Longarm said. "And seeing as you're married to Wild Bill's boy, you know just as good as I do that when your husband's pappy was alive he got hisself a pretty bad name."

"I ought to know!" Mabel Longley exclaimed. "Wild Bill hadn't been in his grave but a few days before I met up with Harland. He'd come here the minute the news spread about his daddy getting hanged, and my folks had a rooming house in town then. He stayed there, and that's how we got acquainted."

"If you don't mind me asking about your own private

157

affairs, why'd Wild Bill's boy come here at all?" Long-arm said. "Or did he just hear his daddy had been caught up with and start out before he found out he'd already been strung up?"

"You've made a real good guess, Marshal Long, and it's pretty close to the mark," she answered. "News about somebody like Wild Bill was spread real fast. Now, the way it was, Wild Bill was living up north in Delta County then. He was laying low, sharecropping with a preacher."

When Mrs. Longley stopped for breath, Longarm said thoughtfully, "That'd be the preacher he killed?"

"Yes," she agreed. "It was the preacher gave Bill away before he died. You see, Bill had trusted him, and told him who he really was. I can't recall right now which one of the names he went under that he was using right then."

"It don't really make much never-mind," Longarm said. "I'd imagine that Wild Bill got real mad at that preacher when the lawmen showed up looking for him?"

"From what I've heard, he did," she replied. "But he made a getaway and got all the way into Louisiana before the law caught up with him. They brought him back to Austin, it being the capital, but they was afraid to put him on trial there because they figured folks would crowd the courtroom and he might have a chance to get away again."

"And that's how he happened to be hanged in Gid-dings?" Longarm asked. "I've wondered about that. Far as I can tell, nobody's ever said a word about how he got brought here."

"Well, however it happened, the news about Bill going on trial had spread around, and Harland found out what was happening and started out for here. The lawmen was in a real big hurry, though. They had Bill all hanged and buried before Harland ever got here. He rented a room at the place where I was staying. He'd been traveling far and fast and needed to rest. But anyhow, that's the way we come to get acquainted."

"I guess I've heard the real story now," Longarm said when Mabel Longley fell silent.

"I'm not sure I could tell you all of it, or that you'd even want to hear it," she said. Her voice was very sober.

"Now, I ain't asking you no questions, Miz Longley," Longarm said quickly. "How you and your husband happened to get hitched up ain't none of my business."

"Perhaps you're right," she agreed. "But I'll tell you this much. Harland set a lot of store in his daddy. Old Wild Bill Longley might have been an outlaw and a careless father, but his son certainly idolized him."

"And when you and Harland was married, you just stayed here in Giddings?" Longarm asked, trying to get off what he saw was an uncomfortable subject for her.

Mabel nodded. "There wasn't much reason to go anyplace else. Wherever we'd've settled, somebody was bound to've found out that Harland was Wild Bill's boy. The folks here already knew it, and after a while they forgot about it, or just as good as forgot."

"Most folks has got a way of being nice like that," Longarm said. "But we've been palavering a long time, Miz Longley. I still got a case to close up, if I'm lucky enough, and I need to get on back into town."

"You're not going to chasing after Harland now, are you?"

Longarm was silent for a long moment. At last he said,

"I ain't of a mind to right this minute, Miz Longley, but there ain't no way of knowing what'll turn up when I get to digging into the case I was sent here on. But I reckon you and me have talked enough for you to know that I ain't one to go off half-cocked."

"Yes, I can see that," she agreed.

"Trouble is, when I'm digging into a case like the one that brought me here, there's times when I feel like my thinker's not much better'n a spavined bronco. I can't move ahead and my neck won't swivel very good to one side or the other."

"Meaning that you don't know where this case of yours—whatever it is—might lead you?"

"That's about the way of it, Miz Longley," Longarm answered. "But I do know I'm going to have to talk to your husband before I can close it up."

"Then I think I'll ride along with you back to town," she said thoughtfully. "And perhaps you wouldn't get angry or think that I'm a nosey, interfering old biddy if I offer to help you any way that I can?"

"Asking your pardon in advance, ma'am, I wouldn't turn away Old Nick hisself if he was to pop up with a puff of smoke and offer me a hand," Longarm replied. "But us standing here palavering ain't going to get no miles put behind us. You'll have a horse to saddle, I'd imagine, so I'll just give you a hand at that little chore, and we'll be on our way."

During the ride back to Giddings in the mid-afternoon sunshine, Longarm did not push his tired horse, and Mabel Longley reined her fresh mount down to a gait that matched his. Neither of them said a great deal; her conversation was limited to naming the owners of the two

160

small spreads they passed and identifying their brands. She asked no questions and volunteered no information about her own situation, and did not once mention the names of either her husband or her son.

Judging by his companion's behavior, Longarm was sure that she had a deeper motive than a desire to lend him a helping hand, but he did not mention his hunch. When the town loomed ahead the sun had left the sky, and by the time they'd reached it and started along its main street, a few lights were beginning to show from the stores that stood in their ragged broken lines. Even from a distance they could see that lights still glowed in the butcher shop.

"Harland or William, or maybe both of them, are certainly working late," she said. "I'd thought sure that they'd have finished by now, but I guess I was mistaken."

"Well, we'll find out soon enough, I reckon," Longarm said as they drew closer to the building. "But I'd bet there ain't nobody inside, or we'd see a horse or two tethered someplace close by."

"I'm sure you're right. But let's look inside, just on the off chance they've tethered their horses behind the building, or even left them at the livery stable."

They'd reached the little shop building now. From their saddles they could see the entire interior of the little store through its wide front windows. A single quick glance was all they needed to see that the place was deserted.

Chapter 13

"Now, that's odd," Mabel Longley said. "If Bill and his father have quit work for the day, they certainly wouldn't've left the store without blowing out the lamps."

Glancing at her face, bathed now in the flow of brightness pouring from the store's windows, Longarm could see that she was truly puzzled.

"Maybe they still ain't finished working," he suggested. "It might be they just knocked off to go get a bite to eat, or maybe to go down to the nearest saloon for a drink."

"They might, of course," she replied thoughtfully. "But neither one of them is what you'd call a drinking man. I'd say it's more likely that they're still out delivering the day's orders to our regular customers here in town."

"That'd make sense," Longarm agreed. "I'd imagine

163

they could save considerable time splitting up and both of 'em working at it. One thing's for certain-sure. They wouldn't've left them lamps burning unless they expected to come back pretty soon."

"It's the only reason I can think of for both of them to've left the store," Mabel agreed. "It still bothers me a bit, though, finding both of them gone and the lights still burning." She hesitated for a moment. "I know I'm imposing, Marshal Long, but could you take the time to go over to the saloon and see if they're there? It's not very far."

"Why, sure," Longarm agreed. "I've already got acquainted with the barkeep. It ain't more'n a hop, skip, and jump, so I'd say it's an off chance that might be where they've gone."

"I do appreciate your help," she said. "And while you're doing that, I'll ride around town a little bit and see if I can catch sight of them. They may still be delivering orders, and I might be able to help them. It's getting late, and we ought to be starting back to the ranch."

"It won't take me but a minute to find out if they're at the saloon," Longarm assured her. "And I'll just look for you up and down the street after I've finished there. In a little town like this one it won't take but a minute or two for me to find you."

Reining his horse around, Longarm rode to the saloon, dismounted, and pushed through the batwings. Somewhat to his surprise, the place that had been empty of customers on his earlier visits now showed signs of life. Four customers stood near the rear of the bar, separated by a few steps from two others, and at one of the side tables near the opposite wall a dignified-looking elderly man was seated, turning cards in a game of solitaire.

McGinty was standing behind the bar, talking to the cluster of four men on the other side of the polished mahogany. He lifted his hand to greet Longarm, and after a few moments broke off his conversation with the quartet of drinkers and started toward him. As he passed the stock shelves at the center of the bar he grabbed the bottle of Old Joe Gideon from the back-bar and scooped up a shotglass. He set the bottle and glass in front of Longarm and gestured toward them.

"Pour your own," he invited.

"Looks like you're managing to keep pretty busy tonight," Longarm commented as he filled the shotglass and sipped the pungent liquor.

"Busier than usual," McGinty said.

"I guess you'd remember if Harland Longley's been in?"

"Of course I would, if he had," McGinty replied. "But he hasn't been. Not yet, anyhow. He's a pretty regular customer too. I keep him a special bottle filled out of my keg whiskey."

"I didn't figure he had, but I thought I'd ask," Longarm went on. "Which ain't neither here nor there. Soon as you got a minute, I need the answer to another question or two."

"You'd better toss your questions at me now, while I'm on hand," McGinty said. "There might be some more customers dropping in that I'd have to look after."

"Whatever you say," Longarm agreed. "First off, I'd like to know if there was anything that sticks in your mind about what-all happened when Wild Bill Longley was caught up with by the law here in Giddings."

Although he'd tried to pose the question casually, as though the matter was one of little importance, Longarm could tell that the barkeeper had been taken off guard. McGinty's jaw dropped as he stared across the bar. He swallowed hard and finally replied to Longarm's request.

"Now, Marshal Long, I'd be very surprised if you didn't know the main thing that happened to him was that he got taken out and hanged. He'd already been tried and found guilty and hanged once, if you don't happen to recall, which I think would be pretty unlikely."

"Oh, sure," Longarm said. "And I know he'd done been strung up once, down in Karnes County. And I know the hanging down there didn't take and he got clean away, just wiggled outa the rope after the lynch party had gone and walked away. But I'm interested in what happened later, here in Giddings."

"Well, I'm not what you'd call squeamish," McGinty said. "But I never have liked to talk about that hanging here. If it's Wild Bill Longley you want to ask questions about, you don't want to be talking to me. Anybody'd tell you I got a special reason not to want to talk about it, because after Wild Bill was dead, old Sheriff Clancey tabbed me to help him and his deputy cut him down. Now, I'm not what you'd call lily-livered, but that's a job I don't want to take on again."

"Then you was close enough to the gallows to see everything that happened," Longarm went on.

"Maybe that's why I never have liked to talk about it," McGinty replied. He gestured toward the table where the solitaire player sat. "Instead of me, you ought to go talk to Doc Barker over there. He was closer to Wild Bill than I got. He stood right by the trapdoor on the hanging platform till Bill stopped kicking. Then he took out that listening apparatus he always carries and stepped up to Wild Bill's body. I don't guess I'll ever forget how it looked, Bill dangling there in the noose, his head all on one side and his eyes glistening white. Doc Barker put his listening piece on old Wild Bill's chest for a minute. Then he turned around and told the crowd he was dead."

"Is that right?" Longarm asked, turning to look at the man absorbed in the cards spread on the table before him. "If he seen every bit of it that close, then I guess you punched the button square when you said he was the man I need to talk to. You don't reckon he'd mind?"

"I don't see why he would. Folks still ask him about it now and then. I guess that was about the biggest hanging that ever happened here in Giddings."

"Well, thanks, McGinty," Longarm said. He fished a cartwheel out of his pocket and laid it on the bar beside the bottle and glass. "I'll be back here to finish my drink in a minute."

Making his way to the table where the solitaire player was sitting staring at his layout, Longarm stopped a half step distant and waited until the doctor looked up. The physician was a small man, but sturdy-looking. He glanced up at Longarm and a frown formed on his face. Longarm spoke quickly before the doctor could object to his solitaire game being disturbed.

"You don't know me from Adam's off-ox, Doctor Barker," he said. "But McGinty told me I oughta come talk to you."

"What's wrong with you?" the doctor frowned. "You look pretty healthy to me."

"Oh, I don't hurt anyplace," Longarm replied quickly. "My name's Long, Custis Long. I'm a deputy United States marshal outa the Denver office, but I'm down here on a special-duty job for Judge Parker, in Fort Smith."

"I'd say you're a pretty good piece from your office and your job both, Marshal Long." The doctor smiled. "But what's brought you over to talk to me?"

"McGinty says he don't like to talk about that hanging, but he told me you're the man that stood by the scaffold on the day when Wild Bill Longley was strung up, the one that made it all legal and proper when you said he was dead."

"That's right," the doctor agreed. "Longley's first hanging wasn't the only one botched up by an amateur hangman trying to handle it. That's why the state passed a law some years back, requiring a certified physician to be in attendance at a hanging and pronounce the subject dead."

"And you was the man that drew the job that time?"

"I did a bit more than that when Longley was finally executed here. I also embalmed his body before he was buried."

"Did you, now?" Longarm said. "Then you sure are the man I'd like to talk to, if you'll spare me a minute from that card game you're playing."

"Well, sit down," Barker invited. "This damned game's not going to play out right anyhow."

Longarm settled into the chair the doctor had indicated, and the physician twisted his own chair around to face him more comfortably. He looked at Longarm, and his bushy eyebrows went up as he asked, "What's got you interested in Wild Bill Longley? He's been in his grave long enough for everybody to've forgotten about him."

"Well, this has to do with the case I was sent here on," Longarm explained. He was fumbling in his vest pocket for a cigar as he spoke. Somewhat belatedly, he looked at his table companion and said, "If you'd fancy a cigar . . . "

"No. I smoke three pipefuls of shag a day, that's my limit," Barker replied. "But light up and go ahead. What's your interest in a dead outlaw, Marshal Long?"

"Why, on this case I been working for Judge Parker, I run into a killing over in Arkansas, it was in a little town called Langley. I'd take it kindly if you don't ask me how it all come about, but from the story I got the killer was all wrapped up in a bed sheet, and somehow Judge Parker's deputy got the idea that he was tied up with Wild Bill Longley. He figured that Longley managed to cheat the hangman twice, and that he's still alive."

"It sounds pretty farfetched to me," the doctor grunted. "Did it make any sense to you?"

"Not a bit. But you know how folks are, when they get all stirred up about something. Now, like I said, this killer was all wrapped up in a bed sheet, like he was a ghost or something."

"Marshal Long," Dr. Barker broke in, "I hope you're not telling me you believe in ghosts."

"Not for a minute!" Longarm replied quickly. "But it ain't what I believe or don't believe. It's what folks that do believe that kind of yarn talks about."

"I don't think I follow you," the doctor said.

"Well, I reckon what I'm trying to say is that it don't take much talk about ghosts walking to get a whole town stirred up," Longarm explained.

"Yes, there's a medical phrase for that delusion, but I won't break into your story to explain it."

"What got me started thinking was that I heard a bunch of jailbirds talking right after I started out on this case," Longarm went on. "They was hashing over

169

what Longley'd done, and some of the things they said just didn't make much sense. That's why I've come all the way here just to make sure. I figured I'd best satisfy myself that when Wild Bill Longley went to the gallows the second time around, he didn't get away like he did the first time he was strung up."

"I'll guarantee you he's dead," Dr. Barker replied. "I not only pronounced him dead on the gallows, I embalmed his body."

"Then I'd say you oughta know."

"Oh, I assure you I do. As I know you're aware, Marshal Long, there's often a case where somebody turns up claiming to be a notorious outlaw who made a miraculous escape from the gallows."

"Oh, sure," Longarm agreed. "That happens a lot."

"That's why I took special care when I was embalming Longley's body. If the rope he had around his neck hadn't done its job, the denatured alcohol and oil of lavender and Venice turpentine and camomile in the embalming fluid that I pumped into him before he was buried would've killed him."

"Granted he's dead," Longarm went on. "Are you certain-sure that it's Wild Bill Longley's body out in the grave he was put away in?"

"Unless somebody's switched corpses since I watched the grave-diggers shoveling dirt on his coffin, Wild Bill Longley's body is certainly in the cemetery out on the edge of town," Dr. Baker told Longarm.

"That's what I was pretty sure you'd say," Longarm observed. He stood up. "And I do thank you for the time you've give me."

"Glad I could be of help," the doctor replied. "Oh— one more thing that I might tell you is that Clint Pawley was constable here then, and he watched Longley being buried too. If you feel like you need another witness, you might stop by and have a talk with him. He lives right down the street, brown house with white trim."

"Why, I figure your word's good enough, Doctor," Longarm assured the medico.

"Well, if you want a sworn statement from me that Longley's dead, I'll be glad to give you one."

"I don't reckon I'll need anything like that right now," Longarm said. "But I'll sure keep your kind offer in mind in case I do. And now I'll just say thanks, and let you get back to your card game."

Turning away from the doctor, Longarm stepped back to the bar. In place of the cartwheel he'd put beside the drink when abandoning it to talk to the physician, there was a small heap of silver coins. Glancing along the bar, he saw that McGinty was in a spirited conversation with the group of men at its far end. Pocketing his change, Longarm finished his drink and stepped out of the saloon into the quiet darkness.

He stopped to light a cigar after he'd pushed through the batwings, and was standing on the edge of the board sidewalk, peering along the dark street, when the thunking hoofbeats of a slowly walking horse broke the night's silence. They came from the center of the town, and Longarm was turning to look, half expecting to see Mabel Longley emerge from the darkness.

Suddenly the tempo of the clopping hoofbeats changed drastically into the rhythm of galloping hooves. Before Longarm could determine the direction from which the hoofbeats originated and turn toward it, a shot cracked. The bark of the shot drowned out the thuds of the hoofbeats as a bullet whizzed like an angry hornet past his head. By the time the slug had thudded into the wall of the saloon, Longarm was drawing his Colt while dropping flat on the sidewalk.

He started rolling toward the edge of the building, seeking the cover cast by its black shadows, and his movement defeated his efforts to determine the location of the hidden shootist. His head was whirling in another rolling turn, and his eyes were looking into nothing but the night's blackness, when the second shot rang out and another ominous dose of hot lead raised splinters from the sidewalk's boards inches from his head.

Before the cracking of the next shot broke the air, Longarm had reached the scanty cover provided by the shadowed blackness that stretched beyond the corner of the building where he'd crawled. After the first flurry of hoofbeats that had given him the first warning of danger, their thudding had stopped as suddenly as it had begun.

Longarm's Colt was in his hand and ready as he began slowly rising to his knees in the concealment provided by the building's black shadows. His eyes were flicking across the small arc that was the only area they could cover from his impromptu refuge. He searched for a target in the darkness beyond the saloon, but the night itself defeated him. Lights were beginning to show along the street from the windows of houses whose occupants had been roused by the gunfire, but Longarm saw nothing except their gleams, no figure of a horseman outlined against their glow.

Boot heels were rapping on the floor of the saloon now as the men inside hurried toward the door. Longarm heard them, but did not turn his head to interrupt his efforts to probe the darkness as he searched vainly for the silhouette of a man on horseback.

Suddenly, even above the clatter from inside the saloon, a wild throaty yell, no words, just a primitive ululating yowling sound, began from somewhere in the shadowed blackness. Before Longarm could attune his ears to its timbre or locate the source of the sound and and turn toward it, hoofbeats drummed on the baked earth again and a blob of grayish white took shape in the deep gloom.

What Longarm saw now was not the figure of a man, but a shapeless, formless shimmer of white three or four times as large as a human body, seemingly suspended in space a yard or more above the ground, and moving swiftly toward him to the rhythmic accompaniment of a horse's galloping hoofbeats. Rising above the thudding of the horse's hooves, a loud wavering yowling unhuman cry began issuing from the strange figure.

For the first time in his lengthy career as a lawman, Longarm stared instead of shooting at a potential target as the disconcerting apparition reached him. The horseman swept past with a thundering of hoofbeats and the wailing of the loud wordless cry. He wheeled his mount just beyond the corner of the saloon building and vanished behind it. The ululating cry that accompanied the ghostly form's passing faded in volume, but was still faintly audible above the shouts of the men whose footsteps were now thunking on the dirt at the corner of the saloon.

Belatedly Longarm realized that in his moment of utter astonishment he had failed to take advantage of an opportunity. He took the two long strides needed to bring him to the corner of the building, but got there only in time to get a final glimpse of the shimmering white shroudlike garment worn by the rider as horse and rider disappeared behind the saloon building's end.

Racing along the side of the structure, Longarm reached the other corner where the strange horseman had vanished. Only a distant pale shimmer of the flowing white garb that had hidden the rider was visible through the darkness.

Longarm's reaction was as swift as usual. He raised his Colt, his gun hand coming up as though drawn by instinct, his thumb seeking the hammer as his arm rose. He framed the indistinct white shape, his thumb levering the hammer back to full cock as he fined up his aim and his finger tightened to squeeze off the shot. Instead of the Colt's normal response there was only the flat metallic thunk of the hammer clacking on a spent shell.

"Damn!" Longarm muttered as he lowered the Colt and memory of his earlier chase after Harland Longley flashed into his memory. "You sure played hell this time, old son, forgetting to reload when you was trying to stop that fellow today! Now you better fork that nag back there and see can you make up for your own jackassery!"

By this time the men in the saloon were pushing through the batwings. Their excited voices such a short distance away masked any further sounds of the horse ridden by the white-draped apparition, and Longarm busied himself by loading his Colt as he waited for the group to reach him.

"What was the shooting about?" the man in the lead asked as he reached Longarm.

"Why, some yahoo rode past and took a couple of shots at me," Longarm replied as he holstered his reloaded Colt.

"I don't guess you know who it was?" another asked.

"Nope," Longarm replied. "But likely I'll catch up with him sooner or later." He was taking out his wallet as he spoke, and he flipped it open to show his badge. "If you'll give this badge the once-over, you'll see who I am. Name's Long. Deputy United States marshal outa the Denver office. McGinty knows about me. You ask him anything else you got on your mind."

"If you're going after that fellow who tried to plant a chunk of lead in you, I'll bet some of us would be glad to go with you. Won't take but a minute to form us up a posse," one of the men volunteered.

"Well, now," Longarm replied, "that's a real thoughtful offer and I thank you kindly for it. But there's only one of him and there's one of me, so if you gents will excuse me, you go on back inside and finish your drinking and I'll get after whoever it was that tried to cut me down."

Chapter 14

Although a swallow of rye whiskey would have been a welcome boon at the moment, Longarm knew that if he went back into the saloon for a quick drink, the men would continue to cluster around him and join in urging him to change his mind. He had no intention of forming a posse. Without exception, each *posse comitatus* he'd led had gotten unruly and required attention to discipline that had intruded on the work its members were supposed to be doing.

As quickly as possible he swung into his saddle and reined his horse onto Giddings's main street. In spite of the commotion at the saloon, only the first few houses he passed showed lights, and one or two of them went dark just as he passed.

Longarm headed for the only place he could think of where he'd find Mabel Longley—the little meat market run by her husband. As he'd thought might be the case, but only half expected, her horse was tethered in front of the small unpretentious building, and through the windows he could see her pacing the floor. Tethering his horse beside hers, he went inside.

"Goodness!" she exclaimed. "I'm certainly glad to see you, Marshal Long. But I was also hoping that you might've run into Harland or William and brought them back with you."

"I was at the saloon, figured they might drop in there, but they didn't," he replied. "And from what you just said, I don't guess you had any better luck than I did."

"Not a bit. I can't imagine what's happened to them, unless they've gone back to the home place."

"I reckon the lights in here was still burning when you got back?" he asked.

"Why—yes, they were," she said. "And of course, if either one of them had come back to the shop since you and I left, they'd certainly have blown them out before starting home."

"Then it stands to reason they ain't been here."

"And it's not likely they'd've started for the ranch without coming by," she said.

"Now the next question is—where'd they get off to? In a little town like this, it ain't likely there's many places where they'd be."

"I can't think of any place. At least, not any place where we haven't looked. You didn't see them at the saloon, I've gone up and down all the streets, such as they are, and . . ." She broke off as a noise sounded outside.

Longarm casually dropped his hand to the butt of his Colt as he said, "That's likely one of 'em coming back now."

"Well, I certainly hope . . ." Mabel Longley broke off in turn as the door opened and a young man came in. Longarm recognized him as being the one who'd waited on him during his first visit to the store.

"I was hoping you'd be here," the youth said. His words were addressed to Mabel Longley. He acted as though Longarm were invisible.

"What's wrong, William?" she asked. Then, hesitantly, she added, "And does it have anything to do with Harland?"

"I—well, I'd rather tell you in private," he replied.

"I don't think that's a good idea," she said. "Marshal Long's told me he wants to talk to Harland. I do too, of course. I want to find out why he acted such a fool and ran away today when he saw the marshal riding up to the ranch."

"Now, William, if me being here's got anything to do with you not wanting to talk free and open, I'll just step outside," Longarm offered. "But I got to tell you, it won't do no good, because when you get finished I'll just have to come back inside here and arrest both of you."

"You can't—" William began.

"Oh, I sure can!" Longarm assured him. "Maybe you better look at it this way. My job here's a sizable piece away from being finished, and I got a hunch that what you don't want me to hear has got something to do with my case. I'd a heap rather help you than hurt you, but I can go either way. Now, you better make up your mind which it'll be."

"Go ahead, William," Mabel Longley urged. "I'd rather keep Marshal Long on our side. Now, I'm as sure as can be that what's on your mind has something to do with Harland, and nobody's got a better right to hear it than I have."

Drawing his shoulders together as though he'd felt a sudden draught of cold air strike him, the youth looked from Mabel to Longarm, then blurted out, "He's gone clean crazy, Harland has! He's sitting out there in the cemetery talking to my granddaddy! And when I tried to get him to listen to me he said he'd kill me if he had to, but he was going to be just like *him*!"

"Oh, my God!" Mabel breathed. "I've been worrying about him because Harland's been acting crazier and crazier for these past few months! From what you've said, he's gone all the way out of his head now!"

Longarm had been trying to make sense of what William had just said, but had been unable to. Turning to the youth he asked, "What do you mean, he's talking to your granddaddy?"

"Just what I said," William replied. "I—well, I— Marshal Long, you wouldn't believe it unless you seen it with your own eyes!"

"I guess I better see it then," Longarm observed calmly. He started toward the door. "Let's mount up, and you take me to where he's doing all this going-on."

"I'm certainly not going to stay behind, Marshal Long," Mabel Longley announced. "Crazy or not, Harland's my husband. If you and William are going to wherever he is, I intend to go right along with you."

"I can't call to mind nobody who's got a better right," Longarm agreed. "But let's all three of us understand something right now. When we get out to where he is, the two of you'll have to wait while I go up close and talk to him."

They'd reached the horses now, and mounted in silence. As they reined the animals around and started off, Longarm went on. "I've smoothed up a few men that's gone off of their hinges, and I got a pretty good idea about what it takes to get 'em back on the tracks again."

"You're not going to hurt Harland, I hope?" Mabel asked.

"Not if I can help it," Longarm assured her. "But there ain't no telling what a crazy man's going to do. He might act gentle as a little baby, but there's as much of a chance that he might go wild and throw down on us and start shooting. So when we get there, I'm going to be the only one that goes up close to him first."

"If he's still like he was, I don't want to go too near him," William volunteered. "I tell you, what he's done is fit to spook out a saint!"

Neither Longarm nor Mabel Longley answered him. They were riding abreast now down Giddings's main street, Longarm flanked by his companions. The street was now silent and deserted. The silence was almost tangible enough to feel, broken only by the occasional yapping of a dog. The night was moonless and a dull cover of clouds blanketed the sky; where the sparse fleeces thinned here and there, faint starlight gleamed.

All of the business buildings were dark, and only a scattered few of the houses showed lights. They reached the saloon. It was as black and devoid of activity as were the houses, with no horses at its hitch rail. After they'd passed the saloon, only a few houses remained between them and the open prairie.

When they reached the point where only the vague outlines of two or three houses were visible in the gloom,

Mabel and William reined away from the road into a fork and Longarm followed them a bit belatedly. Now the road was in much worse shape than the stretch they'd been traversing. It ran through an expanse of rutted barren soil. Here and there the hump of a big rock broke through its surface.

"How much further we got to go?" Longarm asked as their horses slowed when starting up a bit steeper rise than they'd encountered before.

"Just a little way, now," Mabel replied. "We'll be in . . ." She broke off and pointed ahead to a small glow of orange-red as she asked, "William, was there a fire going when you were here before?"

"Yes'm, he started it," the youth replied. "But it was a bigger one than that."

"That's where it was burning, though?" Longarm asked.

"Oh, sure," William answered. "It's in exactly the same place. That's it, all right."

"We'll go a mite closer," Longarm told them. "Then I want both of you to rein in and don't move till I call you."

"If you're going up to that fire, I'm going with you!" Mabel insisted.

"Now, ma'am, just hold on to your patience a minute," Longarm said. "Right now we ain't got no idea about what somebody getting too near that fire's likely to run into."

"But, Marshal Long!" Mabel protested. "That's my husband by the fire there! I'm sure it is! And he'll listen to me a lot sooner than he will to you!"

"I don't aim to argue with you, ma'am," Longarm replied. "But I been in this exact same situation a few

182

times before now, and I got to handle it the way I know is best."

They'd been moving steadily ahead while they talked, and a frown had formed on Longarm's face as they drew closer to the faintly glimmering firelight, for he could now make out the shapes of two men inside the small circle lighted by the flickering beams. His frown deepened when he saw that one was draped in white, while from the small amount of detail that he could make out by the dim reddish light of the little fire, the second man's garb was a long, tightly fitted dark suit.

"We'll stop here," he said sharply, reining in his horse as he spoke and dropping quickly out of his saddle.

"But, Marshal Long!" Mabel protested. "Don't you see the same thing I do? That's Harland all draped in a bed sheet, all right, but there's another man with him by that fire. And it can't be . . . ." She stopped short, her eyes fixed on the little blaze, then she gasped, "Oh, Lord bless us! It can't be, but it is! It's him in the flesh!"

"I reckon we're seeing alike, ma'am," Longarm replied.

"Then let me go with you, Marshal!" William said quickly, before Mabel Longley could speak. "My pappy showed me how to handle a gun! I might not look like it, but I can throw down on a man with a pistol as good as anybody and better'n most!"

"I've already told Miz Longley, and I'll tell you the same thing," Longarm replied. His voice was sharply commanding. "I want both of you to stay right here. And starting right now, don't either one of you do anything but what I tell you to!"

Without waiting for a reply, Longarm swung out of his

183

saddle and dropped the reins of his horse to the ground so the animal would stand. He started toward the small fire, taking small steps and placing his feet on the ground slowly and carefully to avoid having his boot soles grate on the hard-baked soil.

Though his glimpses of Harland Longley during Longarm's cross-country chase at the ranch had been both distant and fleeting, there was no possible way that he could be mistaking the bulky form of one of the men beside the tiny blaze. The bed sheet in which Harland was wrapped clung closely to his bulky body and did nothing to hide the fact that he was grossly, almost impossibly, fat.

Harland's pudgy arms protruded from the sheet's folds; they looked like small hams, and his hands would have served as sofa pillows. The sheet in which he was draped did not cover his face. It was a double bulge of cheeks that dwarfed his small rounded nose and squeezed his eyelids until they appeared as small slits. Below the almost-invisible knob of his chin a waterfall of double chins descended to his chest.

Each step that Longarm took revealed a new bit of detail on the visage of the motionless man across the fire from Harland. He appeared to be leaning half-erect on some sort of prop that supported his back and shoulders. He was hatless, and the firelight's glow revealed his face in full detail. It was an unusually narrow triangular face, with a high protruding forehead bulging from a puffing tangle of black hair.

His eyes showed only as deep wells of darkness in the dim uncertain light. His face was narrow, with high cheekbones that extended below his eyes and shadowed them. He had an overlong flared nose, while a thick sweeping black mustache and full beard hid the lower portion of his elongated thin face.

"Old son," Longarm muttered in an almost inaudible whisper as he moved another careful step closer. "There ain't no such things as ghosts, but if there was, you'd sure be looking at one! That's the same face you seen on that wanted flyer you handed over to the Texas Rangers when you was in Austin. And it can't be, because Wild Bill Longley's been dead and in his grave going on ten years now!"

In his preoccupation with examining the face of the motionless man across the small fire, Longarm had not paid close attention to the ground he was traversing. His boot sole slipped on a loose stone, and though the noise it made was slight, the scraping sounded loud in the silent darkness.

With a speed of movement that was astonishing, the sheet-shrouded man leaped to his feet. The sheet dropped away as he stood up, clawing at the holster on his hip. Even in the dimness the size and bulk of his grossly fat body surprised Longarm, but he had neither the time nor the need to complete his examination of the fat man.

Before the rising man could bring up his revolver, Longarm's Colt roared its message of death. The heavy slug from the revolver struck the fat man before he could level his own weapon. The pistol sagged in his hand as he tried to level it, and the spastic death-grip of his fingers triggered off a shot. The slug did nothing except kick up the dust a yard from Longarm's boot tips. Then the fat man crumpled slowly, a sagging fall that left him on the ground in a huddle, the Colt in his hand dropping as he collapsed.

• • •

185

Stretched at ease in Chief Marshal Billy Vail's private office, Longarm looked across Vail's paper-littered desk at his chief. Before replying to Vail's question, he flicked a match-head across his thumbnail and puffed one of his long thin cigars alight.

"Well, you see, Billy," Longarm said, "there wasn't but one way to go about closing that case, even if you don't agree with what I done."

"I suppose you did what you had to," Vail said. "But I haven't heard yet from Judge Parker. I just hope he's satisfied with the way you handled it."

"He oughta be. That fat Longley ain't going to go parading as a ghost no more and shooting the judge's deputies."

"Oh, I'm sure you did the best you could," Vail replied. "To give you credit, Long, you always do. But it seems to me that if you'd been all that positive about Harland Longley killing that man in Judge Parker's jurisdiction, you could've just arrested him and let a judge sentence him all legal and proper."

"Billy, when Harland Longley shot that fellow in Langley, he was all bundled up in a bed sheet so's nobody could see how big and fat he was. Now, how's anybody going to make a case against a man nobody ever seen?"

"Well, I'll have to admit you've got a point there," Vail agreed. "And at least your case is closed."

"I'm glad you see it my way, Billy," Longarm said through a cloud of smoke that he'd created by puffing on the long thin cigar clamped in his lips. "And I'll bet you that Wild Bill Longley's just about the only outlaw in the country that's come out of his grave and set off another outlaw on a killing spree. And I wouldn't mind putting a bet on something else either."

"What's that?" Vail asked.

"Why, you oughta see that easy, Billy. Wild Bill Longley's the only outlaw that's ever been hanged twice before it took."